DEATH ENTERS THE CONVENT

A CHARLOTTE EDGERTON MYSTERY

Adele Fasick

MonganBooks

SAN FRANCISCO, CALIFORNIA

Book Layout ©2013 BookDesignTemplates.com

Cover design by Kit Foster Design.

Death Enters the Convent/ Adele Fasick. -- 1st ed.
ISBN 978-0-9853152-7-6

In memory of
Janet Mongan
1931-2017

CHAPTER ONE

A Troubled City

*I awoke this morning with devout thanksgiving for my friends,
the old and the new.*
  Ralph Waldo Emerson

March 5, 1849—Florence, Italy

Charlotte woke with a start of fear as she heard the childish voice murmuring, "Rock-a-by, rock-a-bye". Sunlight crept in through the slightly parted curtains over the long, Italian windows. Turning her head, Charlotte looked at Daniel still sleeping peacefully, his hand thrown back over his forehead. She leaned closer to kiss his shoulder before sliding her feet down from the bed and standing up.

Lifting Margaret Mary from her infant bed, Charlotte walked into the kitchen, shutting the door firmly behind her. Today would be a test. At least it might give her a clue as to what her future could be.

Today her friend Abigail was arriving from Boston with her new husband and her son. Would Abigail be beaming with happiness or would Charlotte see telltale signs of discontent on her face? After many years as a widow, a husband would change her life. Would Abigail still remember old friendships? How much would Abigail tell her about her new life? And how much could Charlotte tell her old friend about the fears that kept her awake at night? Abigail, always serene and unworldly, had never been troubled by an urgent need for money.

A knock on the door a few hours later signaled the guests' arrival. Abigail looked almost the same as she had back in Massachusetts—neat in her deep blue dress and unadorned bonnet. Her son Timothy was now a tall fifteen-year-old with unruly dark hair. His eyes were as bright and his smile as cheerful as Charlotte remembered from when he was an eight-year-old pupil in her class. With them was a tall, gangly young man with close-cropped black hair looking solemn in his dark gray jacket. Abigail introduced him as Marcus Talbot, a recent Harvard graduate and Timothy's new tutor.

But Charlotte's eyes lingered longest on the fourth figure in the group. Tall, solidly built; his black jacket and vest brightened by a discreet blue cravat, Abigail's new husband, Robert Baxter, exuded the dignity of a successful Boston businessman, a powerful publisher who might change Charlotte's life. He bowed slightly toward Charlotte as Abigail introduced them.

Daniel came out from the study and joined the introductions. After asking about their trip, he turned to Timothy. "What's this I hear about your wanting to be an artist? You have certainly come to the right place to study."

"Indeed we have," Abigail answered while Timothy reddened and nodded his head. "The sight of Florence as we drove over from Leghorn was overwhelming. The churches are unlike anything I've ever seen. I was almost afraid the carriage would tip over when we all leaned toward one side to see the top of the cathedral dome."

They laughed as they sat down at the table set on the balcony of their flat. Margaret Mary's nurse, Maria, had prepared tortellini with sardines. "Now I am sure we are not in Boston," Abigail remarked.

Margaret Mary waved a sleepy good-by as Maria carried her off to her nap. Robert Baxter was soon questioning Daniel about the book he was writing. As one of the most successful publishers in Boston, Charlotte knew his opinion of Daniel's work was important. She tried to hear the men's conversation even while she listened to Abigail.

"How can Daniel bear to stay in his study and write?" Abigail asked. "Living in this beautiful city must make you long to spend hours roaming about looking at all of its treasures."

"That is what I have been doing," Charlotte admitted. "Studying Italian and walking around the city while Daniel has been resting and getting over his cough." She didn't mention the fear that Daniel's cough aroused in her. What would she ever do if she lost him? How could she live if anything happened to him? And how could she take care of Margaret Mary?

After ending their meal with coffee and pastries, Robert Baxter left to call on the American consul, Lewis Cass, to talk about banking arrangements with him.

Charlotte and Abigail led the young people out into the sunshine, walking arm in arm down the busy, narrow street. Marcus and Timothy trailed along behind, stopping every few minutes to stare at a small shrine built into a wall or the curve of an arch over a doorway. Abigail was silent, her head turning from side to side as she tried to absorb the details on the stone walls along the way, finally she breathed a deep sigh and spoke.

"My Quaker eyes have never seen art like this. Look at the blue of the Madonna's robe in that roundel over the door of the house on the corner. Who would ever think of having sculptures and paintings in doorways? There are religious symbols at every turn. It's almost more than I can take in."

"It is overwhelming, isn't it?" Charlotte was sympathetic. "This city is filled with people who can't stop making pictures—paintings, statues, wall reliefs—

they are everywhere. Americans have no idea of the riches of Italian art. But we turn here at the piazza. Now we are getting close to one of my favorite places."

They crossed a quiet square toward a church and entered a low building next to it. First through a dark entranceway and then into a burst of sunshine as they emerged in a green cloister. Suddenly everything was quiet. Birds chattered in the small trees around the green lawn. The gentle music of a choir floated from the chapel. Women's voices rose and fell in unison. Charlotte led Abigail toward the stone wall under the sheltered cloister walk where they could sit on a bench and listen to the soothing sounds. Even Timothy was subdued as he and Marcus walked slowly around the walls examining the carvings.

The music of the choir faded away and a group of six nuns wearing brown habits and black veils walked slowly out of the chapel and toward another door on the side of the cloister. Their hands were clasped in front of them and their eyes were downcast, but one woman stood out in the group. She was not a nun, although she wore an old-fashioned flowing nun-like habit. Her gown was dark blue rather than brown, and even the veil that covered her hair was blue. Unlike the nuns, she did not keep her eyes cast down modestly at the ground but looked around her as she walked. When she saw Marcus and Timothy, she frowned slightly and then glanced at Abigail and Charlotte briefly before turning back to the two young men. As the nuns approached the door, Charlotte saw her pause for a moment and stare fixedly at Marcus before she turned her head and followed the others inside.

"What is the name of this place?" asked Timothy as soon as they were outside on the street again. "Were those women in the strange dresses all nuns? I've never seen a nun before."

"This is the Santa Chiara Convent," Charlotte explained. "Most of the women you saw are nuns. But I don't know about that woman in the blue dress. She was different somehow."

"Yes, she was different," Abigail joined in as they walked slowly out of the cloister. "I'd like to know more about those nuns and their lives. What would it be like to live in a beautiful convent surrounded by art and beauty? But do they never go outside? Italy is so different from America. It will take time for us to get used to it."

An abrupt shout from the other side of the piazza startled them. Moving closer they could see men milling about the street. Many of them carried signs proclaiming "Grand Duke Leopold" or "No elections— no foreigners". Some of the demonstrators had green bandannas tied around their heads. Many had luxuriant mustaches and as they raised their arms and shouted, they looked like pirates threatening to take over the road. Charlotte translated the signs for the others as quickly as she could.

"The people are protesting having elections," Charlotte explained.

"I never heard of people opposing elections," said Timothy. "Why are they doing that?"

"Some of the radicals who have been opposed to the Grand Duke want to declare a Republic. But many of the common people love the Grand Duke and don't want him to go. Many of them cling to their local language and local ways. They don't want to join with other provinces to make up a country. They want to remain Florentines. They think people who live in Venice or Naples are foreigners."

"Well, I have to admit," said Marcus, "Virginians sometimes seem like foreigners to those of us who live in Massachusetts. Perhaps we are not as different from Italians as we think we are."

Their discussion was interrupted as the shouts grew louder. A column of soldiers wearing blue jackets with red collars and carrying long rifles entered the square. The leader lifted his sword in the air and ordered everyone to disperse while his troops fired several shots over the heads of the crowd.

Charlotte seized Abigail's arm and urged her to hurry away from the confrontation. Marcus led the way, sweeping his arm to disperse the people blocking their path and Timothy trailed behind reluctantly, turning as often as he could to see what was going on.

Gunshots continued to rumble as they left the piazza. Three unshaven men, their green bandannas bright around their heads, were being forced away from the area by soldiers on horseback. The soldiers shouted something and one of the men picked up a stone and hurled it at his horse.

As the horse reared and whinnied, Charlotte and Abigail pressed themselves against the wall of the nearest building. Amidst the shouting and running, the soldiers and their quarry disappeared from the piazza. Within a few minutes Charlotte and her friends reached a quieter street.

Abigail paused to catch her breath. "Well, Italy is far more exciting than I had expected. We came here for a quiet time of study, but it looks as though we are in the midst of another revolution. Do you think there will be more trouble tomorrow?"

"These are difficult times for Italy. Trouble seems to haunt the country," Charlotte replied. And trouble is haunting me too, she thought to herself, but I'm not ready to talk about it.

CHAPTER TWO

An Assignment

A room hung with pictures is a room hung with thoughts.
Joshua Reynolds

The next morning Charlotte strolled to the palazzo where Robert Baxter had rented a large apartment for the family—Abigail, Timothy, Marcus, and Elsie, the housekeeper who had come with them from Boston. Charlotte enjoyed walking through the peaceful streets with Margaret Mary. Now that the election was over, quiet had descended on the city. Elderly women with shopping baskets on their arms paused to smile at the child and one of them handed her a sprig of violets. A grave priest in his cassock looked up from his breviary and signed a blessing.

When she arrived at the lodgings, Charlotte was ushered into an entrance hall with high ceilings and several paintings on the walls. The reception room where she and Abigail sat down to have coffee and pastry seemed palatial to Charlotte, but when Elsie, the housekeeper, brought in a tray of coffee and fresh biscuits, the aroma was just like Boston. Elsie clucked over Margaret Mary just as Charlotte's mother would have. Memories of the many austere meals she and Abigail had shared at Brook Farm swept over Charlotte.

"Robert has business in the city," Abigail began. "That will give us a chance to catch up on all that has happened since we last visited together."

Charlotte relaxed in her chair. A chance to talk to a sympathetic friend from home was just what she longed for. Her worries came tumbling out.

"Daniel has such a terrible cough! I don't know what to do. The doctor in England could offer nothing except to tell us to go abroad. He looked so gloomy, I just know he was thinking there was little hope." Gulping back tears, Charlotte fell silent.

"Sunshine is the best cure for a cough." Abigail spoke quietly as Charlotte paused.

"Yes, and Daniel's cough is getting better. I am sure it is." Charlotte seized on the hope. "But he worries about finishing the book he is writing. It is a biography of the Irish hero, Wolfe Tone. He has already been working on it for months and there is much more to do. Some days he is too tired to pick up his pen. That troubles him and makes his cough worse

"Now his sister writes to say his mother is ill and needs money for medicine. We would like to send money, but I scarcely know where I can find it."

"Perhaps I can help…" Abigail started, but Charlotte quickly interrupted.

"No, no. I must take care of this myself. And I do have some good news. The day before you arrived, I had a letter from Horace Greeley."

"The newspaper editor?"

"Yes, the editor of the *New York Herald*. He wants his paper to be a journal of world affairs, not just American news. Our friend, Margaret Fuller, has been a foreign correspondent for him and she recommended me. In his letter, he asks me to write articles about Florence and explain why it attracts so many American artists."

"They are flocking here, aren't they? Horatio Greenough, I've heard, has set up a studio. And other painters and sculptors are joining him."

"Indeed they have. Mr. Greeley wants me to tell people about the American artists here, but he also wants me to write about the city and politics. He would pay well. Daniel would not have to worry so much. It would help us both if I were able to earn some money."

Margaret Mary had long since climbed onto her mother's lap and fallen asleep, still clutching part of a biscuit in her hand, but a clatter of footsteps on the stairs interrupted the women's quiet talk and woke the child. Marcus soon entered the room and Timothy behind him, his face rosy with enthusiasm.

"You should see Signor Bagnoli's studio where I will be taking classes, Mother," he said as soon as he had greeted them. "It overlooks the Arno, so the light comes streaming in. He showed us some of the pictures his students have painted, pictures of flowers that look so lifelike I could almost have picked them off the walls. He said I'd have to start by drawing, not painting, but after I learn to do that carefully enough, he will teach me to use paints."

Margaret Mary had slipped down from her mother's lap and now ran over to Timothy, who took her hands and swung her around in circles. She squealed with delight. Marcus stood back watching them and looking rather awkward.

Charlotte turned to him and asked, "And what did you think of the class? Was it the delight of art that drew you to Florence?"

"No, Mrs. Gallagher. I had a rather more personal search to make. Many years ago, just before I was born, my father's sister, my Aunt Isabella, married an Italian man in Boston. My grandfather was so opposed to the marriage that he disowned his daughter and refused to speak to her new husband. The young couple returned to Italy and their names were never mentioned in my family. It was only when my father was dying last year that he asked me to try to find his sister. He regretted the long estrangement."

"Ah, and do you know where your aunt is living now?"

"I am afraid not, although her husband was originally from Florence. I believe she might be in this city or nearby. Her husband's name was Pietro Onofrio, so I will search for him while Timothy makes his pictures."

That evening, after Margaret Mary was in bed, Charlotte had a chance to tell Daniel the story of Marcus's Aunt Isabella.

"I believe I have heard the name of Pietro Onofrio," Daniel said. "He was one of the freedom fighters who wanted Tuscany to become more democratic and the Italian states to band together. The Italians have been fighting for democracy far longer than the Americans fought for it, but they haven't been as successful."

For the next few days Charlotte and Abigail spent hours together visiting some of the historic churches of Florence. There seemed no end of places to visit, but Charlotte was determined to make a start on her first article for Horace Greeley without wasting too much time. She decided that Americans would be interested in hearing about Santa Chiara and its art treasures, many of which were unknown to outsiders. One afternoon she walked resolutely toward the convent. Instead of entering the public areas, she rang the small bell attached to a wooden door at the side of the cloister.

As the door squeaked open, Charlotte saw a small nun who looked like a child playing at being a nun in her heavy robe. When Charlotte explained that she would like to speak to the abbess about the convent and its art, the nun answered in a gentle, childlike voice that the abbess was very busy.

"You had better talk with Sister Dolorosa," she advised. "She will be able to tell you all about the history of the convent and answer all your questions."

When Sister Dolorosa appeared, her wrinkled cheeks and stooped shoulders made Charlotte wonder how many years she had spent in the convent. Looking up at Charlotte with bright brown eyes, the nun smiled and murmured a greeting.

Charlotte was grateful for all the weeks she had spent learning Italian as she returned the greeting. "Good morning, Sister Dolorosa. I wonder whether I might ask you some questions about Santa Chiara and its beautiful paintings. I would like to tell Americans more about your historic building."

Sister Dolorosa led Charlotte into the small chapel where the nuns sang their morning and evening prayers. The usually smooth white walls were marred by ugly scars.

"Oh, Sister, what has happened?"

A quiet shrug of shoulders and a lifting of eyebrows was the nun's only answer as she led Charlotte to the back corner of the chapel. A large statue of a Madonna and Child had partially slipped from its pedestal and now rested at an awkward angle against the wall. Charlotte could almost feel the reproachful eyes of the Madonna on her.

"This is terrible! What has caused such destruction?"

"During our blasphemous election, protestors fired guns to prevent people from voting. Our beloved Santa Chiara must have wept as she looked down from heaven. The election was a mistake, but no one should shoot guns so wildly and attack sacred property. Our abbess will have to visit the bishop to make arrangements to have this statue placed on its pedestal again and the walls repaired."

"Oh," sighed Charlotte, relieved, "I hope the repairs will soon be made."

The nun turned her attention to the statue of Santa Chiara standing close to the main altar. "At least the ruffians did not attack the statue of our patron saint. Her statue and the beautiful chalice made especially for her feast day are among the greatest treasures of the convent."

"May I see the chalice?" Charlotte asked.

"The chalice is only on display for Santa Chiara's feast day, when mass is celebrated in her honor. But that day is only a few weeks away now. This year the bishop himself may celebrate the mass in her honor."

After seeing the chapel, the nun led the way to a small room lined with shelves holding old books and rolled scrolls of parchment. Several small pictures hung on the walls between the bookcases and the window. One showed a Madonna and Child seated on a rock outside a dark cavern in what appeared to be the desert.

Charlotte lingered longer over the next one, an elaborate drawing of the earth with the sun and planets circling around it.

"That is one of the oldest pictures we have in our convent," Sister Dolorosa explained. "It has hung in that spot for 500 years or more.

"The nuns must have taken very good care of it for all those years, as they did for all of the books." Charlotte glanced around the library as she spoke.

"Yes," the nun agreed. "We have taken good care of the pictures and books. And the good God has helped us. Santa Chiara helps us still. Sometimes at night she has been seen in the library, looking at the books. She is guarding the convent against false and heretical books and pictures."

Charlotte smiled at the faith of the elderly nun, but she was surprised when the nun spoke again, this time in a strongly accented English. "I speak your language a little. I have taught myself from the books and writings that I have tended for these past forty years. Those of us who serve the Holy Church must understand the thoughts of others."

With words and gestures the nun invited Charlotte to seat herself at the heavy oak table in the center of the room and look at some of the books shelved around the walls. Then with a nod of her head she left the room to return to the chapel and join other nuns chanting their prayers.

After an hour poring over the intricate Latin script in heavy leather volumes and examining tiny illuminations, Charlotte's eyes were tired. She wondered how much detail her readers would want about the rites of the Catholic Church. The sound of music from the chapel had died away by the time Charlotte left the library and began searching for Sister Dolorosa to thank her.

As she walked across the cloister grass, Charlotte watched the nuns emerging from the chapel into the sunshine. They walked in the same orderly line as they had before, but suddenly one of the nuns stumbled and seemed about to fall. Two of her companions quickly lifted her and helped her walk into the building, but the nun appeared to be quite weak.

When Charlotte found Sister Dolorosa and told her she was leaving, she asked about the nun who had almost fallen.

"Oh, it was nothing," answered the elderly nun. "Sister Felicita has a slight touch of consumption. We will say special prayers for her tonight."

By the time Charlotte got home to Daniel and Margaret Mary, she was worrying again about the article for Mr. Greeley. How could she explain the beauties of colorful illuminations to people who had never seen any pictures except crude black-and-white newspaper illustrations?

"Oh, Daniel, how am I ever going to give anyone an idea of all the things I have seen in Italy?"

Daniel's pale face lit up when he heard that. "Now at last you know how difficult the journalist's life is. This is what I have been struggling with for years. But you will do it, Charlotte. I have faith that you can do anything you set your mind to."

The sound of Margaret Mary's laughter and chatter in the next room put an end to the conversation. Dinner was followed by a rest for Daniel and the child, but Charlotte, unused to the habit of an Italian *riposo*, had not yet learned how to sleep during the middle of the day. She struggled to record in her notebook the ideas and feelings raised by the pictures she had seen.

Her task was interrupted when Maria brought her a note left at the door. It was from Abigail, just a few scrawled words, "News has arrived that will change our plans. I had been so looking forward to a nice, long visit in Florence, but perhaps that is not to be. I will call on you tomorrow morning to tell you more."

CHAPTER THREE

Meeting Isabella

You will begin to wonder that human daring ever achieved anything so magnificent.
John Ruskin

While she waited impatiently for Abigail's visit the next morning, Charlotte spent more time trying to describe Florence for her American readers. Would she be able to explain to a housewife who had lived all her life in a small Maine village the size and age of a city that had existed for centuries? The broad sweep of the River Arno carved the city into separate neighborhoods, each one with its own character. The stone walls of the buildings along the river were covered with ancient lichens and water marks from floods no living person could remember. Even the paving stones on the streets were scarred by wagon tracks laid down centuries ago. Boston and New York seemed harshly new in comparison. Charlotte struggled to find words to bring the city's beautiful streets and buildings alive for her readers.

Finally Abigail arrived. Her usually serene brow was creased into a frown. As soon as they had exchanged greetings, Abigail burst into speech. "My plans to see more of Florence will have to be postponed. We expected to stay here for a month or more before leaving Timothy to his studies. Now, unexpectedly, my husband's business interests have called him to Rome. He wants to meet with several authors whose work he may publish. I will go with him, of course, and we expect to be there for several weeks perhaps even a month or two. I have been longing to see the Roman ruins I have read about, but I expected a somewhat more leisurely trip. It will be difficult to move on so quickly.

"Isn't there still a lot of unrest in Rome because of the defeat of the Republican forces?"

"Yes, I believe that is true, however, my husband's colleague writes that the streets are quite safe for Americans. Troops are drawn up before the papal palace, but they are not threatening to people going about their daily business. Americans do not usually become involved in European wars, as you know. Most foreign visitors do not learn Italian and scarcely understand what is happening. Timothy might be tempted to join the rebels if we took him with us, but he will stay here and continue his studies with Marcus.

They have Elsie to keep house for them and see that they eat properly."

"At least I will be able to write to you often," Abigail added. "Lewis Cass has asked my husband to send him news about what the Americans in Rome think about the new governments forming in Italy. I am sure my letters to you can be included in his pouch."

Abigail's visit was a short one. She hurried off to do her packing, promising that they would see each other before long.

Timothy and Marcus joined Charlotte when she returned to Santa Chiara a few days later. The monastery cloister was fresh and green and a few violets had appeared around the bases of the statues. Calm music floated from the chapel door as the nuns sang their canticles. The three of them watched the line of nuns leave the chapel and walk toward their cells behind the cloister and once again the woman in the deep blue dress followed behind them. As Marcus glanced toward her, she hesitated in her walk and then stopped and frankly stared at him. She turned again to follow the nuns, but seemed to change her mind and looked toward Marcus again. Finally she left the pathway and walked toward the small group in the cloister.

Bowing her head slightly toward Charlotte, the woman greeted them in Italian, but switched to English when she heard Charlotte's accent as she returned the greeting. "Ah, I thought you might be English, or perhaps American? You may think it strange that I should speak to you without an introduction, but I am an American myself and you interest me greatly."

Turning toward Marcus, the woman continued. "You have a striking resemblance to my brother, whom I have not seen in many years. His name is Richard Talbot and he lives in Boston, Massachusetts."

"You must mean my father. I am sorry to have to tell you that he died more than a year ago. I am Marcus Talbot. You must be my Aunt Isabella, who left Boston when I was a small child. During my father's last illness, he spoke of you often and told me that someday I might find you in Italy. I never thought it would be in a place like this."

Isabella Talbot, or rather Isabella Onofrio, grasped Marcus's hands and held them tightly as he introduced her to Charlotte and Timothy.

"I thought I saw you here a few days ago. It took me a while to realize why you seemed so familiar, but when I saw you today, you looked almost exactly like my brother. It is many years since I have seen any of my family. I have been afraid to return to America because my father disowned me so vigorously. He told me that if I married Signor Onofrio I would be betraying my family and should never return to Boston again. And I defied him."

"Grandfather has been dead for more than five years," Marcus said. " I can assure you no one else in the family feels that way. We would welcome you home. One of the reasons I came to this country was to try to find you."

"We are very happy to meet you Signora Onofrio," Charlotte added. "I am Charlotte Gallagher. We used to live in Boston too. My husband and I have become friends with Marcus and I would like to invite you to join us for dinner. Are you a nun? I am afraid I am not sure what the rules of Santa Chiara are. Is it possible for you to leave the convent and visit us?"

"Oh yes, Mrs. Gallagher. I have not become a nun. I am a boarder in this convent, which I find a very peaceful place to live. I am free to leave at any time and to mingle with lay people. It is generous of you to invite me to dinner and I am happy to accept the invitation."

On the day of the dinner, Marcus and Timothy walked to Santa Chiara to accompany Isabella Onofrio back to their lodgings. The short walk gave them time to become acquainted with Marcus's aunt. Although she lived in a convent, she was not as quiet and subdued as Marcus had expected. She was lively and quite talkative as she asked many questions about her newly discovered nephew and his friends.

"You were quite right to come to Florence to study painting," she told Timothy. "There is no city in the world where you will find better teachers. The streets are filled with art, so even the humblest peddler becomes aware of the glories of painting and sculpture.

America has no city to compare with it. Don't you agree?"

"The only city I have ever seen is Boston, and certainly that looks nothing like Florence," Timothy admitted. "The art is wonderful, but Americans want to develop their own art."

"Well, American artists may want to forge their own art," laughed Isabella, "but when I see how many of them are here in Italy copying the old paintings and sculptures of the masters, I cannot help but think they realize they still have much to learn. And what of you," she turned to Marcus. "Are you studying to be an artist too?"

"No, unfortunately I have no talent for art. My task is to help Timothy continue his studies so he can attend Harvard College when we return to Massachusetts. And while I am here I want to learn as much as I can about Europe, especially Italy."

Daniel and Charlotte welcomed their guest and the party was soon seated around the dinner table. Isabella wanted to know all about what was happening in America. And she was eager to hear about Daniel's newspaper work in London. By the time dinner was over, she seemed like an old friend. Gradually she started telling them the story of what had happened to her after she left Boston.

"My husband and I went to New York after we were married. He had been exiled from his native Italy because of his revolutionary activities. When his enemies fell from power, we returned to Florence, where my husband had been born. He was very happy and so was I. His family was welcoming. They did not object to his marrying a Protestant and indeed we finally had another wedding in a Catholic church, as they had wanted. It was a lovely celebration quite unlike the secret marriage we had in Boston before we left the country."

Isabella leaned back in her chair and smiled happily as she remembered those days. Then she continued her story. "At that time, Tuscany was a democracy and my husband was welcomed as a supporter of the new Republican government. We had many friends some of them members of the governing council. Everyone was glad to have Pietro Onofrio home and to meet me as his wife. When our son was born, our happiness knew no bounds. We named him Giovanni after my husband's father. He was a happy, healthy child and we had no worries as far as I could see. But I was oh so wrong.

"All of the governments of Europe were opposed to democracy, especially for the Italians. My husband wanted to see a unified Italy all the way from Savoy down to Naples, but the Austrians claimed the northern provinces and the Pope ruled all of the central area. Suddenly people who had been eager for democracy were turning against it. Some of them accused my husband of leading them astray. It was a terrible time. And we were expecting our second child, so I was tired and feeling ill."

Isabella twisted her hands in her lap and Charlotte leaned toward her to say, "You do not have to tell us more. Please do not upset yourself.".

But Isabella insisted on continuing. "My husband sent me away to visit an aunt of his who lived in Assisi. The air was good, but that trip was the worst thing that ever happened. The fever came to that city and our little Giovanni became sick and we lost him. Then a week later I lost the baby I was carrying. I was in despair.

"All this time there was a struggle here in Florence to see who would take over the government. My husband tried to stand up for democracy, but he was distracted by trying to take care of me as well as his parents. The last time he visited me at his aunt's house, he told me, 'We will win, Isabella, you shall see. If anything happens to me, my family will take care of you. And when everything seems lost, remember that Santa Chiara will save you.

"That was the last time we talked. He left to return to Florence and I never saw him again. Neither has anyone been able to tell me for certain what happened to him. His father lived only a few months after Pietro left, and his mother died of a broken heart not long after that. I found refuge at the convent of Santa Chiara. Although I feel no calling to be a nun, it is a peaceful place to live and I am as happy as I could hope to be."

The small group of listeners had been silent as she talked. When she finished, Marcus cleared his throat, "Now that I have found you, perhaps you will want to visit your family in America. There are not many of us left, but after all the trouble you have seen in Italy, you might want to return to your old home."

"Perhaps someday I will want to do that. But it would be difficult for me to leave Santa Chiara now. The nuns have been kind to me and they are facing uncertain times."

"Because of the damage done to their chapel by the radicals?"

"Not only that. The bishop has recently said that he may take their convent away. There are Dominican monks who lived in that convent many years ago. They were expelled more than a century ago because they had grown lax and immoral. Now they say they have reformed and want to return to their original home. Some people say it is because Florence has become so wealthy that they could amass greater treasure here than they hope for in their present monastery in the mountains."

"That is outrageous!" Daniel interjected.

"It seems so to us Americans, but Italian law is very different from ours and bishops have a great deal of power. Besides, the current bishop was once a Dominican monk and has close ties with that order. I do not think it is fair. I love the convent and would like to help the nuns keep it. They are respected in the community and help many people."

"You could not have found a more beautiful place to stay than at Santa Chiara," Charlotte agreed. "I guess that is what your husband meant when he said Santa Chiara would save you."

"That is what I always thought he meant," Isabella agreed. "Recently I have wondered whether he meant something more." She interrupted herself with a laugh. "Oh, perhaps I think too much about the past. You are all young people. We must look toward the future and see what that will bring."

After their guests had left, Charlotte and Daniel talked for a while about what a pleasure it was to see a family reunited.

"It's strange she is satisfied to spend her life in an Italian convent," mused Charlotte. "I expected she would leap at the chance to go back to Boston and the life she knew there. Now that her husband and child have died, what is it that ties her to Italy?"

"Yes, I was thinking the same thing. Those last words that she remembers her husband telling her— that she would be saved by Santa Chiara—are mysterious. Does she believe she has to spend the rest of her life there? She does not seem like a superstitious woman."

"She said she had changed her mind about what her husband meant by those words, didn't she?"

Daniel frowned thoughtfully. "Something has happened to make her suspect there is more in Santa Chiara than she realized. Would that have anything to do with Marcus? What else has changed?"

CHAPTER FOUR

Starting the Chase

In the middle of the journey of our life I came to myself within a dark wood where the straight way was lost.
    Dante Alighieri

"I beg pardon for disturbing you so early in the morning, Mrs. Gallagher, but I am deeply worried about Mr. Marcus." Elsie Brown, Abigail's housekeeper, burst into speech as soon as Charlotte opened the door. Her bonnet was a trifle askew and she clutched her small handbag with white-knuckled fingers. Charlotte quickly gestured her inside. Timothy was with her but he let Elsie do the talking.

Elsie continued in quick bursts. "Last night Mr. Marcus told us—Timothy and me—that he wasn't feeling well and wanted to get some fresh air. When he did not appear this morning for breakfast, I knocked on his door good and loud. I thought he had slept late. But

31

there was no response and I soon discovered his bed had not been slept in. What could have happened to him?"

Elsie walked over to the window and looked out as though she expected to see the young man. A light rain was falling and a chilly wind blew across the piazza. The few people walking across the square had their heads bent against the wind.

"Does Marcus usually let himself into your lodging when if he is out in the evening? Has he a key? Did you hear him come in?"

Elsie shook her head. "Usually the portiere lets us into the building, but he willingly gives a key to any tenant who expects to be out late. Mr. Marcus would have taken a key, I am sure. I certainly did not hear him come in last night."

"There is probably some simple explanation for this, " Charlotte reassured her. "Perhaps Marcus just became lost and could not find his way home. Of course it is possible that wandering about late at night he might have encountered a thief. Was he carrying any valuables, do you think?" Without waiting for an answer she continued, "We had better start looking for him."

Daniel was soon enlisted to start the search. He suggested that Charlotte should take Margaret Mary with her and wait at the Baxter's lodgings with Elsie. Meanwhile he and Timothy would walk around the local streets to look for any traces of the young man.

They could ask some of the shopkeepers whether they had seen a young American or whether they had heard of an accident during the night. Margaret Mary's nurse, Maria, could go with them to help with translation.

It was easy to find people who might have seen Marcus. Peddlers walked up and down the narrow streets with baskets filled with bread, fish or flowers. Daniel tried to describe the tall, thin American youth they were searching for and Maria translated as quickly as she could. They learned very little, although several people were happy to engage in conversations.

At the nearby market, they asked one elderly woman selling flowers, "When you came here early this morning, before the sun was up, did you see a tall young man—an American on the streets?"

"No! No Americans here," the plump, cheerful woman replied. "Americans do not like the crowded streets of the city but ride through on their carriages paying no attention to people here."

"This young man would not be in a carriage certainly. He is a poor student without the money for carriages," Daniel told her.

"Ah well, then I will say a prayer for the poor young man. Perhaps some wicked thief tried to rob him. Or some of those revolutionaries who are fighting against the Grand Duke might have attacked him. There have been many street brawls recently. But Americans do not often become involved in our local struggles. I will say a prayer to the Blessed Mother for your friend."

The man in the fish stall next to the old woman's chuckled when they asked him about seeing a young American man. "Ah, this is Italy! Surely there is nothing strange in a young man wandering out at night and not returning to his home. He met a beautiful young woman, no doubt. That is what youth is for. Ah, I can remember..."

Daniel silenced him with a frown, while Timothy was staring at Maria wondering what the man would say next. Daniel spoke to Maria too, "Tell him this is not a romantic escapade. Young Americans like Marcus do not wander off with beautiful women in the night."

After more than an hour of fruitlessly questioning people on the street, Daniel, Timothy, and Maria walked over to the river and asked some of the boatmen about accidents. No one had seen a stranger near the river the night before or in the early morning when they were bringing in their catch.

"Look!" Timothy cried, pointing toward the back of a tall, thin figure walking quickly down the cobbled street next to the river. "That looks like Marcus!"

Even as he spoke the man turned into a narrow alley between two somber gray buildings on the other side of the street. Timothy sprinted after him with Daniel following and Maria trailing along behind.

Timothy was hot in pursuit and kept gaining on the man, who looked back over his shoulder and then increased his speed. He ran frantically into yet another alley and when Timothy followed, he saw the figure dodging behind a peddler's cart. Just as the man tried to turn into another street, he slipped on the wet pavement and fell heavily on the cobblestones. Timothy caught up with him quickly.

"Marcus, Marcus, it's me!" Timothy cried. But when the man turned his face toward the boy, Timothy quickly realized he was a stranger. Feeling sheepish and guilty, he helped the man up from the pavement and mumbled excuses in English, which the stranger clearly did not understand.

By this time Daniel and Maria had caught up with them. They were both winded, but they quickly saw what had happened. Maria exploded into an excited burst of Italian attempting to explain Timothy's chase, but the man merely scowled at the three of them.

"He had no idea why you were running after him," Maria explained. "I think he ran because he might have stolen that loaf of bread and was afraid he would be caught. He speaks no English and has no idea of this 'Marcus' you are chasing. That is what he says."

Daniel was embarrassed by their mistake, and Timothy's cheeks were red. He had been sure he would be a hero for finding Marcus, but instead he had led them all on a wild goose chase. Daniel gave the man a few coins to make up for the trouble they had caused him, and then they turned back to the piazza. For all the excitement of the chase, they had accomplished nothing. Daniel began to wonder whether Marcus might have been kidnapped and was being held for ransom.

"We should go to the hospital near the Dominican Abbey," Maria suggested. "Perhaps, if the young man was injured, a kind soul would take him there."

The monks at the Abbey smiled and responded kindly to Maria's questions, but they knew nothing about a young American man. After a lengthy conversation, Maria turned to Daniel, "Brother Anselmo says that no young men are in the hospital. The holy monks take care of sick elderly people. No one has been brought there for several days. He said he would pray for the young American's return."

Daniel and Timothy had to be satisfied with this. The noon hour had passed and the city was shutting down for its *respito* time. Although the rain had almost stopped, drops still sprinkled down from the sky and rivulets of water ran down the faces of the stone angels in their niches along the street. Timothy wondered how the sculptors could have carved faces that smiled serenely on sunny days but seemed to weep when the rains came.

Charlotte and Elsie had spent all morning worrying and waiting. Daniel's somber face when he and Timothy returned told them the news was not good.

"We could not discover a trace of Marcus," Daniel told Charlotte. A coughing fit interrupted him, but he continued with determination. " I will visit the American consul's office when it reopens this afternoon and see whether any inquiries have been made. I wonder whether Marcus was carrying any letters or papers that might let a stranger know where he was staying. It is unlikely that whoever found him would be able to read whatever papers he might have. But even if they did not read English, surely they would recognize the language and try to find someone who could help."

Charlotte urged Daniel to stay home and rest, but he insisted on walking with her to the office of the recently appointed American consul, Lewis Cass Jr. When they reached the stately building that housed his office, they were ushered into a dim, gloomy room. Heavy velvet drapes hid most of the windows and equally dark upholstered chairs were scattered around a fireplace. Behind the imposing desk, sat a broad-shouldered man in a formal, dark blue suit peering at what appeared to be a dozen or so letters on the desk. He rose and walked around the desk to greet them.

"Good afternoon, Mr. Gallagher, I believe we have met before. You are the young man who is writing a biography of that Irishman, are you not?"

"Yes, indeed I am. And this is my wife. We are worried about a friend of ours, a young American who seems to have disappeared. Last night he went out for a walk and did not return.

"This morning we searched through the neighborhood asking whether anyone had seen a young American wandering about. We found no trace of him. We asked questions of the ferrymen on the river, but no one has fallen into the river or had any other accident that they know of. We are very concerned about his welfare."

"I hope this young man has not been tricked into getting involved in any criminal or unsavory behavior. As you may know, there were some disturbances at the cathedral square last night when a group of radicals attempted to nail anti-papal notices to the church door."

"I find it hard to believe Marcus would have allowed himself to be tricked into doing anything he would be ashamed of," Charlotte said quickly.

As they were talking there was a discreet knock on the office door and a young man entered. He handed Mr. Cass a note and waited for an answer.

"Ah, perhaps this mystery is being solved as we are sitting here," exclaimed Cass. "This note is from a local citizen who would like to speak to me about a young American man he has met. Let us see what he has to say". He turned to his secretary, "Please bring Mr. Tanassi in."

The man who entered the room with the secretary appeared to be a gentleman. His black trousers and gray jacket were well-cut and of fine material. He was of medium height and his luxuriant hair was sprinkled with gray. He walked with a slight limp, but he looked youthful and his small, neat beard was glossy black. He gave a slight military bow to Cass, who then introduced Daniel and Charlotte.

Mr. Cass opened the conversation. "My secretary informs me that you are seeking information about a young American man who, you say, you rescued last night. I have asked Mr. and Mrs. Gallagher to meet you because I think they may be seeking the same person. Please tell me about the man you rescued."

Signor Tanassi was not to be rushed. "Well, I must explain how these strange events occurred and why it took me so long to make a report," he said. "My name is Lorenzo Tanassi, and, as I wrote in my note, I am a native of Florence and an artist. Yesterday I had dinner with a friend at his palazzo. There were disturbances in the street last night, so I lingered longer than usual with my friend. It was late when I walked home and the streets were quiet. Suddenly I heard someone call out, 'Help me!' I was startled to hear the voice, especially because the man was calling in English. I hurried to the corner and saw that someone had stumbled and fallen on the steps of the small chapel on Via Cortina.

"When I went to help the man up, I saw blood running down his cheek from a cut on his forehead. I ran over to help him up and realized he was quite young and seemed feverish as well as dazed and confused by his fall. When I asked whether he could get home all right he answered 'How far is it to Brattle Street?' That answer made no sense, so I decided to take him to my own home and let him rest for a bit. I live near the Piazza Mentana. "

"Did the young man recover when you reached your house?" asked Charlotte eagerly. "Was he able to tell you his name and where he lived?"

"When I got him home, I realized he was feverish and in no condition to talk, so with the help of my housekeeper, Signora Patti, I bandaged the cut on his head and put him to bed in a spare room. Unfortunately, when morning came he had not completely recovered. The wound on his face was healing, but his fever had grown worse and he became a bit delirious. I had business appointments, but my sister and my housekeeper, generous women that they are, nursed him through the morning. By the time I returned home, his fever had abated and he seemed more himself, although he remained pale and weak. He told me that his name was Marcus Talbot and that he was working in Florence, however, he could not give me a clear description of where he was living. When I asked about his parents, assuming he was travelling with them, he told me that both his father and mother had died and he was living with another family."

Relief flooded Charlotte as soon as she heard Marcus's name and realized they had discovered where he was. "Oh, I am so glad that he is safe. I had been fearful that he might have been seriously injured or lost."

CHAPTER FIVE

Finding New Friends

A friend is a person with whom I may be sincere.
Ralph Waldo Emerson

The Gallaghers thanked Lewis Cass for his help as they left his office with Signor Tanassi. They were greatly relieved to have found Marcus, but the afternoon was growing dark and a chill rain was starting to fall again. Charlotte could see that Daniel's cough was troubling him.

"If Mr. Tanassi does not mind, it might be best to wait until tomorrow to visit Marcus," she suggested to Daniel. "Then perhaps Marcus's aunt will be able to come with us. I am sure she will be worried about the young man."

"That is an excellent suggestion," Signor Tanassi agreed. "Mr. Talbot is young and strong. A few days rest will find him well again, but he should avoid this bad weather. My sister and I will be happy to welcome you to our home tomorrow,".

Charlotte sent a note to Isabella telling her the news and the two women met the following morning. When they arrived at the Tanassi Palazzo, they found an old and elegant house with rather bare walls of brownish stone and a massive door that led into an airy courtyard decorated with several sculptures and stone benches.

Signor Tanassi met them in the courtyard and led the way up a stone staircase and into a large parlor. Marcus was lying comfortably on a sofa near a sunny window, his legs covered by a light blanket.

"Oh, Marcus, what a fright you gave us," Isabella said as she walked toward him. He struggled to stand up, but she waved him back. "Do not get up now," she urged. "You are still feverish and need your rest."

As she spoke, a tall, spare woman in a black dress glided into the room carrying a tray on which stood a bottle of wine and some glasses. She quickly put the tray down on a table and looked at the guests expectantly.

"This is my sister, Signora Alma Rizzo," Lorenzo introduced her. "She has been taking good care of your friend Marcus."

Marcus was rather pale, but he sounded cheerful as he told his story. "I was feeling feverish and a bit dizzy the other afternoon. Timothy and I had spent several hours reading Latin and I was tired of being cooped up indoors. I decided a walk in the cool evening air would be just the thing.

"I started walking toward Santa Chiara to see what it looked like by moonlight. The night was so beautiful that I walked longer and further than I had expected but had not reached Santa Chiara. Finally I realized I was lost and very tired and I turned to go back the way I had come. But that is where I got into trouble. The streets twist and turn so much that I found myself going in circles."

"Yes, our Florentine streets can be very confusing," agreed Isabella.

"When I entered the square by the Duomo," Marcus continued, "I saw a group of men clustered around the church door. I decided to ask for directions, but unfortunately I was interrupting a bitter argument. When I walked toward them, one man turned toward me and raised a knife threateningly. As I dodged to evade his blow, I lost my footing and must have fallen on the stone steps."

Marcus paused for a moment and then continued, "I must have been unconscious for a while. The next thing I remember was opening my eyes and seeing a strange man leaning over me. That of course was Signor Tanassi. I tried to speak to him, but was unable to form a word."

"He was unable to say anything coherent," agreed Signor Tanassi. "But I took his arm and managed to get him here and into bed. He fell into a deep sleep and did not wake until late in the morning."

"Yes, and when I woke up, I didn't know where I was. Signora Rizzo was sitting by the bed and I tried to ask her a question, but her answer sounded like a riddle. I could make no sense of it. I remember thinking I should go back to Harvard to attend my classes, but nothing looked familiar and I didn't know the way home."

"By the time I came home," Signor Tanassi added, "the fever had lessened and Marcus was able to tell me his name and let me know that he was staying in Florence. But he was still somewhat feverish and confused and could not remember the name of the piazza on which he was staying. Fortunately all I needed to know was that he is an American. Then it was easy to decide to visit Mr. Cass and ask about him. Meeting you in the office was a stroke of luck."

While this conversation was going on, Marcus was growing more and more tired. His head drooped and Charlotte could see his eyes were closing. Signora Rizzo noticed too and spoke swiftly to her brother who nodded in agreement.

"My sister says that your Marcus must rest another day or two. The scratches on his face and hands are not deep, but his fever could be dangerous if he does not rest. Travellers often become sick when they visit Italy. Perhaps it would be best if he stays here until he is completely well rather than trying to go back to his lodgings. Why don't we let him sleep now for a while and I can show you the rest of the house? You might be interested in the paintings in my studio."

In a few minutes the visitors were seated in the sunny studio while the housekeeper brought tea and cakes for them. Charlotte and Isabella were impressed by the number of portraits scattered around the room. Near a large window stood an easel with a half-finished picture of an attractive young woman with two small children leaning against her lap. The woman's face was almost completed and her large, dark eyes gazed serenely at the viewers, but the two children were only lightly sketched. Clearly the picture was still a work in progress.

As they talked, both Charlotte and Isabella began to feel quite at home with Lorenzo Tanassi. He told them about his father, who had served in the army of the Grand Duke Leopold, ruler of all Tuscany. Lorenzo had hoped to become a soldier like his father, but he had broken his leg when he was young. Although it healed, it never became perfectly straight again, so he had to give up his army plans. He turned to painting and achieved some success as a painter.

"But my father was never quite satisfied," Lorenzo admitted. "My brother was called to serve God, but my father wanted me to be a worldly leader. He thought being a painter was no work for a gentleman. If I couldn't be a soldier he wanted me to be a diplomat, so he wrangled a small position for me in the Grand Duke's court. I spent my time writing letters and carrying out missions for the duke and his courtiers. It was tedious work. After my father's death, I resigned that post and became a portrait painter."

"I believe you might have painted a portrait of my husband's father," Isabella said. "His name was Giovanni Onofrio. My husband treasured that portrait."

"Ah, Signora Onofrio. I am charmed that you are familiar with my work. If you should ever want a portrait of yourself, I would be honored to undertake the task."

"I am afraid I am not eager to have to look at a picture of myself, Signor Tanassi. My life now is very quiet. I live with the nuns at Santa Chiara and seldom entertain visitors. I am happy in my modest, nun-like life and have no desire to display a portrait."

Over the next several days Isabella and Timothy called often upon the Tanassis. They read to Marcus and Timothy told him about what he was doing in his art classes. Lorenzo Tanassi often joined them. He asked Isabella many questions about Santa Chiara and the art works that were stored in the chapel.

"I have heard that there are other treasures in the convent—hidden perhaps."

Isabella frowned as she replied, "Why would the nuns hide the beautiful art that some of the finest families in Florence have given to them over the centuries? My husband's family commissioned a magnificent statue of the Madonna and Child as a thanksgiving for the miraculous cure of their son and heir. It has stood in the chapel for more than three hundred years although it was recently damaged by the guns of a mob."

Lorenzo's eyes searched Isabella's face. "Ah, but over the years there have been many struggles in Florence. This is not the first time we have had fighting in the streets. Heretics and rebels have often appeared in Florence. There may have been times when the nuns feared for the safety of their treasures."

"It is true, I believe, that some of the gifts of the Onofrio family have disappeared from the convent," Isabella admitted. "My husband told me once that he would like to go through the collection to see whether he could find records of some of them. But he certainly did not blame the nuns for their loss."

"Secrets beg to be discovered," Lorenzo said. "And there is much wickedness in the world. Sometimes it even finds its way into convents."

"I have heard about the Bonfire of Vanities here in Florence," Timothy exclaimed. "That was when the monk Savonarola burned pictures and books he thought were heretical."

"Do you think the nuns of Santa Chiara would have sinful art or heretical documents?" Isabella stood up, her skirt swirling with the haste of her movement. "I find that difficult to believe. But we will not argue. It is time for us to go, Timothy. We will come back tomorrow to see Marcus. Perhaps by then he will be ready to return to your lodging."

Alma Rizzo linked her arm through Isabella's as the two women walked toward the door. "You must forgive my brother for his curiosity," she said. "He grieves for the loss of any of the treasures of Florence."

Isabella nodded her head in agreement but did not smile. "There are many stories about what has happened in Florence and many accusations about the mysterious loss of priceless paintings and statues. The nuns of Santa Chiara are among the most innocent inhabitants of the city. Surely they should not be the targets of such accusations."

When Isabella visited Marcus on the following day, she found him eager to return home. His fever was gone and he was growing tired of being treated as an invalid. Lorenzo and his sister insisted on taking Marcus back to his lodging themselves. Alma brought a basket of Italian delicacies for him—to keep up his strength—she explained. Marcus was glad to be home and to submit to the fussing of Elsie and enjoy the nourishing soup she had made.

As the Tanassis were leaving, Lorenzo once again begged Isabella to consider letting him paint her portrait. Isabella shook her head in refusal, but Charlotte noticed that she did not seem displeased by the request.

Marcus refused to play the invalid. "The women have fussed over me enough. I am quite well now. Tomorrow we will start on your studies again," he told Timothy.

A few minutes later they were interrupted by a knock on the door and Charlotte walked into the room. "I had to see with my own eyes that you had arrived safely" she told Marcus. "You may miss some of the luxury of the Tanassi palazzo, but no doubt you will be glad to taste good Boston brown bread again."

While Charlotte chatted with Marcus and Timothy, Isabella walked to the window and stared out at the patch of river visible between the church tower and the palazzo across the piazza. When Timothy led Marcus into the library to show him the sketches he had been making during the past week, Isabella turned to Charlotte.

"How is your article for Mr. Greeley coming along? Are you discovering all of the secrets of Florence and enlightening your American audience about them?"

"Secrets? I am afraid I have not been privileged to discover any secrets about Florence. My article will, I hope, open the eyes of my readers to the sights and sounds of the city, but you undoubtedly know all about them."

Isabella sighed as she sat down on an ornate chair near the window. The sharp gray light of the afternoon revealed small wrinkles near her eyes and the beginning of worry lines around her mouth. She was older than Charlotte had realized, or perhaps the losses she had suffered had aged her prematurely. Was her usual serene expression a mask to hide the pain she had endured losing her husband and family? Charlotte felt a stab of pity. But she must listen to what Isabella was saying.

"Have you been studying each of the landmarks of the city? Perhaps you have read some of the history books that tell of our heroes and our wars. What have you read of Santa Chiara?"

"Not a great deal. Sister Dolorosa showed me the library at the convent, but the books are very old and difficult to read. My Italian is not as good as I would wish. It would take many months to go through those books. I will rely on tales told by people who have lived at the convent. People like you and the nuns. I doubt that Santa Chiara has many secrets."

Isabella stood up so abruptly that Charlotte caught her breath in surprise. What had she said? What was wrong? After a long pause, Isabella said quietly, "I must tell you what I have discovered. There are more secrets than I ever dreamed of."

Charlotte stared speechlessly as Isabella moved toward the door. "Please call upon me at Santa Chiara tomorrow. Perhaps we will be able to talk about secrets."

CHAPTER SIX

Secrets Everywhere

To happy convents, bosomed deep in vines, Where slumber abbots, purple as their wines.
Alexander Pope

Despite the brilliant blue of the Italian sky and the sunlight brightening the trailing bougainvillea on their balcony, Daniel shivered as he picked up his mug of coffee. Charlotte's heart tightened when she heard the familiar hack of his cough.

"Why don't you sit on the balcony and enjoy the sun for a while?" she suggested.

Daniel's frown deepened. "I must finish my book," he muttered despairingly as he made his way slowly back to his study. The supply of money draining from their bank account was almost visible to both of them like drops falling from an emptying rain barrel during a dry spell.

A few minutes later Charlotte made her way again to Santa Chiara and told the shy young nun who answered the door that she wanted to see Signora Onofrio. Isabella soon appeared and invited her into her small, neat parlor. Whitewashed walls set off several charcoal drawings arranged on the wall above a sturdy table.

"What a lovely, peaceful room," Charlotte exclaimed. "Those drawings are striking. They are very much like some of the drawings in the library."

"Yes, I believe they are by the same artist as some of those in the library, Antonino Pellarosa," Isabella agreed. "The drawings are only sketches and are not signed, but the style is similar to some frescoes Pellarosa painted for the chapel. The convent has so many lovely drawings that I borrowed these for my private room."

Charlotte took a seat at the table and Isabella placed in front of her a package wrapped in dingy cloth.

"When the shots of the demonstrators caused the Madonna statue in our chapel to fall from its pedestal," she explained, "I found this document hidden beneath it. Where it came from I do not know, but I discovered it just after the statue crashed to the floor. The nuns were still at their evening meal and heard nothing, but it sounded quite loud to me. I ran into the chapel and saw what had happened before anyone else got there. At first, I thought I should show these pages to the abbess, but something made me hold onto them until I could examine them carefully myself."

Isabella smoothed the sheets of paper as she laid them on the table. Edges were curled and one corner was torn off, but the writing stood out clearly. The words were Italian, written with dark, thick strokes. The women squinted, trying to make sense of them.

"Oh, there is a date—All Saint's eve in the year of Our Lord 1642." Isabella's voice faded as she tried to decipher the scrawled words.

"It looks like a list," Charlotte observed, "and there are other dates. But what do they mean? What happened on those dates?"

The two women sat close together at the table, their heads bent over the papers. A knock on the door startled them and Isabella quickly threw her arm over the papers, her wide sleeves hiding most of them, as she called out, "Come in, come in."

The door opened slowly and a pale young girl in a novice's robe peered around it without entering the room. "Sister Dolorosa sent me to ask you whether you would like me to bring you and your guest some coffee." Her soft voice was almost lost in the sound of the nuns' voices as they chanted their prayers in the chapel nearby.

"Ah, I lead such a quiet life, I had not thought of my duties toward a guest. Please join me in a cup of coffee."

Charlotte hesitated, but Isabella continued. "You must allow me to show you some Italian hospitality. If we were in Boston it would be tea and biscuits, but here in Florence we love our coffee." She smiled at the waiting novice and accepted the offer of refreshments. Charlotte noticed how the young girl's eyes swept over the half-hidden papers on the table as she turned to leave.

When the novice had left, Isabella slipped the papers into a large wooden chest. "We can talk about what this list means, but it would be best not to let other people see it before we do."

The coffee arrived, dark and steaming, and with it several small apricot pastries. Charlotte watched the young novice as she arranged the plates. The girl frowned and set each plate carefully on the table. She held the coffee cups so that not a drop was spilled. Her mind was surely not on a dingy old pieces of paper, Charlotte thought. She is scarcely more than a child trying to be a grown up nun.

As if she had read her thoughts, Isabella turned to Charlotte as soon as the novice had left the room. "You no doubt think me foolishly suspicious when I hide the papers from our novice, Lucia. She is young and childlike, it is true, but her family has been entwined with this convent for centuries, just as the Onofrio family has been."

"You must be very devoted to the convent to have decided to spend your life here," Charlotte said.

"You wonder why a protestant New England woman would choose to live shut behind convent walls—of course you do. Even when I came here, I had no idea I would live here so many years."

"I do not mean to pry," Charlotte hastened to say.

"You cannot help but wonder. Well, I will tell you. After I realized that Pietro had disappeared, his parents were very good to me. His mother treated me like a daughter and we clung to each other during our grief. When Pietro's father died, we wept some more. But soon his mother had gone too and I was left alone."

"That must have been difficult."

"Oh, yes it was. I was neither a widow nor a spinster. There was no place for me in Italian society and I had no home to go to in America. The money in Italian families is always left to men, so Pietro's uncle controlled what was left of the family fortune. He is a cardinal in Rome and I imagine that his nephew's American wife was an embarrassment to him. He told me he would provide me with a generous allowance if I would live in a convent—the only respectable place for a single woman to live."

"That must have been very hard for you. I had no idea you were forced to live here."

"At first I felt sorry for myself and could think only of how I could arrange to leave. I still hope to build an independent life for myself, but I am not alone. Many of the nuns here have come because they have no choice. Some families have too many daughters and cannot find husbands for all of them, so they send the unmarried daughters to the convent. But most of the nuns are well-educated and independent women. We have time to read and write as well as to serve the people in the neighborhood. I cannot accept the superstitions of their religion, but I enjoy sharing their work. We provide care for the sick and elderly as well as finding homes for orphans and neglected young people. Even my American friends would approve of our work."

"It sounds as though you have found congenial friends," Charlotte said. "And are many of them, like Sister Lucia, from families that have deep roots with Santa Chiara?"

"Florentine history is an elaborate labyrinth of families who have married and quarreled and fought for centuries. Americans have no idea how long people's memories are here. Nothing is forgotten in Florence. Deeds that were done three hundred years ago are as alive in people's minds as though they happened last year.

"Remember I told you my husband said Santa Chiara would always save me. At first I thought he was talking about a spiritual saving, or comforting. He was not a religious man, but he knew that if anything happened to him I would be shaken to my core and would need consoling."

"He must have been a loving husband to have thought so much about taking care of you after his death." Charlotte's breath caught and she was swept by a sudden fear of what would happen to her if Daniel were to die and leave her. No! That would not happen. But Isabella was talking again.

"As the months and years passed, I began to wonder whether he was speaking of a more worldly saving. When the Medici ruled Florence more than three hundred years ago, the Onofrios were an important family. They gave many treasures to Santa Chiara over the years. Several Onofrio women, daughters and widows, spent their lives in this convent. Duke Ferdinandus Onofrio commissioned artists to paint a set of the stations of the cross for the chapel, and goldsmiths to make sacred vessels such as candlesticks and chalices."

"You must enjoy seeing those treasures now. Almost like having a remembrance of your husband."

Isabella stood up and paced the floor restlessly. When she turned back to Charlotte, her face was white and strained.

"I have never said this to anyone before, but to you I will say that the comfort of those treasures is less than I had expected. When fire destroyed the Onofrio palazzo, all of the paintings and small statues that survived were transferred here. But no one is sure which gifts were given by the Onofrios. And there have been questions about the quality of some of the works. Have some of the originals been given away or replaced by copies? Some of the gifts may have been lost or given to churches or private patrons who keep them in their own houses. It troubles me. Those works were created to be shown in churches and chapels where they could inspire all people with thoughts of religion—not for the private pleasure of wealthy patrons."

"Does the convent have a list of where all of their gifts came from? Of the families who gave them?"

"I have been told that each bishop keeps records of church property."

"Oh, that makes it easy, doesn't it? You can ask the abbess to show you the records of the works of art here at Santa Chiara."

"Alas, the abbess…"

A gentle knock on the door interrupted their talk. The novice, Lucia, appeared again and spoke to Isabella. "Sister Dolorosa would like to know whether your visitor will join us in the chapel for prayers."

Isabella turned to Charlotte with an inquiring smile and was met with a shake of the head and a few stumbling words about leaving to return to her husband and child. Isabella waved her hand impatiently at Lucia. "Please tell Sister Dolorosa that Signora Gallagher is leaving but I will join the nuns in the chapel in a few minutes."

After the novice left, Isabella handed the package of papers to Charlotte. She spoke urgently.

"Please take these and see what you can make of them. Perhaps you can unravel some of the secrets of

Santa Chiara. You might even share some of them with Americans in your article."

Margaret Mary was sleeping comfortably in her bed when Charlotte reached her lodging, and Daniel was bent over the desk in his study. Books were scattered across the table, some open, others closed, piled in stacks of varicolored leather. His pen scratched steadily at the pages in front of him.

"Ah, I wish I could write as quickly as you do," Charlotte complained with a smile. "Your book is coming along well, while my article creeps like a snail. Will I ever finish it? And just when I thought I had gathered all of the material I needed, I discovered a mystery about Santa Chiara. If I could add that to my article, Mr. Greeley would surely be impressed."

Charlotte told him about what Isabella had said about the strange, old notes she had discovered. She laid them on the table for Daniel to see.

"It is a list, isn't it?" Daniel said. "A list of numbers. They seem to be dates. But what are the words next to them?"

"The writing is old-fashioned and difficult to decipher. And some of the words are almost illegible. I hope Isabella and I will be able to read them eventually. I have a feeling that these dates might lead to fascinating discoveries. Santa Chiara is a mysterious place."

CHAPTER SEVEN

Santa Chiara's Feast Day

Love of beauty is taste. The creation of beauty is art.
Ralph Waldo Emerson

After a restless night, Charlotte woke to the sound of rain on the windows. Margaret Mary was sitting up on her small bed contentedly pulling strands of yellow yarn from her doll's head. "Oh, you'll have a bald dolly soon if you keep that up," warned Charlotte, but the child only laughed and kept pulling at the strands.

The rain didn't keep Maria Spinelli from arriving and setting to work in the kitchen. Maria also brought a letter that had been delivered by courier. Charlotte was cheered when she saw it was a note from Abigail. She opened it quickly.

My dear Charlotte,

Thank you for the note telling us of Marcus's misadventures. My husband and I are very grateful that you and your husband were able to rescue the poor young man. It seems that he fell into benevolent hands and had a very happy escape from the dangers that lurk in Italian cities.

Our trip to Rome is going well. Every day in Rome leads to the discovery of something new to look at and admire. Seeing St. Peter's Basilica for the first time was an overwhelming experience. Every day I take my sketch pad to one of the churches and try to capture the beauty of the sculptures and frescoes. My abilities are small, but I believe they are growing with all the practice.

We have also made new acquaintances. Most of the guests in our boarding house are English or Irish people who find the Italian weather more friendly than British chilliness. Two elderly sisters from Dublin, Miss Anne and Miss Violet Osborne, share my love of art and we have sometimes gone together on sketching outings. They introduced me to a monk named Dom Giovanni, a Dominican, who guided us to one of the smaller churches in Rome where we have found lovely examples of 16th century Italian frescoes and sculptures. The Misses Osborne have been most congenial acquaintances.

Meanwhile my husband is busy discussing the possibility of publishing Italian literature in America. He is looking for translators who might be able to help with this project.

Ah, but now the courier is becoming impatient to leave. I must end this letter with much love and best wishes for you and your family. Please write again when you have the time. We do not want our newly revived friendship to wither.

Your faithful and grateful friend,
Abigail Baxter

By the time Daniel got up and joined Charlotte and Margaret Mary, the kitchen smelled of fresh-baked bread and the whole family gathered around to enjoy the heat from the brick oven.

"You had better not go outside today," Charlotte sighed. "I don't want both you and the baby to catch colds. There's enough coughing in this house as it is. But I would like to go to Santa Chiara to see the celebration of the saint's feast day. I'll wait a while and see whether the rain stops."

An unexpected knock on the door startled all of them. It was Alma Rizzo. "Ah, Mrs. Gallagher, I wonder whether I might accompany you to Santa Chiara today to see the feast day festivities. I have seldom been to that convent and would like to know more about it. The Tanassi family has for many years supported the good work of the Santa Chiara convent."

Brisk winds were pushing the clouds across the sky and the rain had slowed to a fine mist as the two women walked to Santa Chiara. When they entered the chapel, they saw that the niche holding the statue of

Santa Chiara was lit with scores of candles to mark her feast day. An ornate gold chalice decorated with a row of diamonds and rubies sparkled in the candlelight. Several nuns knelt on the floor below the statue and murmured the words of a litany to Santa Chiara.

Chiara most faithful, pray for us.
Chiara most obedient, pray for us.
Help of the weak, pray for us.
Comforter of the afflicted, pray for us.

Charlotte and Alma watched the nuns as they finished their prayer and began to sing a hymn. Charlotte noticed the young nun she had seen faint while walking in the cloister. She still looked pale. Even as Charlotte watched, the nun slumped over toward the side and slid to the floor. There was a gasp that rustled through the small congregation and then a large, strong nun half carried the young nun out a side door and toward the convent cells. The mass continued without a pause.

Isabella was sitting in a pew toward the back of the chapel. When the mass ended, she smiled at Charlotte before turning to leave. As Charlotte and Alma stood outside, under the shelter of the cloister arcade, Isabella joined them.

"What happened to that poor young novice who fainted?" asked Charlotte. "I saw that happen once before. She must be quite ill."

"I am not sure," Isabella hesitated. "Sister Assunta, the tall woman who serves as our cook, looks after her and she is assigned easy tasks in the library so she does not get too tired. But I think the time has come for her to see a doctor. The home remedies that the nuns prepare do not seem to be helping. However, I am sure the abbess will arrange for that."

"I have never seen a more beautiful chalice," Alma remarked as though she wanted to change the subject. "Is that one of the gifts of the Onofrio family?"

"I believe so," Isabella answered. "There is no official list of their gifts, but my husband once told me that many years ago they gave a remarkable chalice to the convent."

"Thank very much for accompanying me here," Alma turned toward Charlotte. "I will leave you now. I recognize the abbess as a girlhood friend of mine and I would like to say a few words to her. I had not realized she was serving at Santa Chiara."

After Alma left, Isabella invited Charlotte to come back to her private parlor for a talk. As soon as they were seated in the privacy of the room, Charlotte asked Isabella more about the gifts the Onofrio family had given to the convent.

"Does the list of dates have anything to do with the Onofrio gifts? The dates on that list start in 1630, do they not, and end some ten years later? Do you have any idea when the Onofrio family started giving the gifts? How old is the chalice?"

"The dates must have some significance," Isabella agreed, " but I am at a loss to figure out where we can get more information about them or about the gifts the convent has received. The Onofrio family was not the only family that gave paintings and works of art to Santa Chiara. Many of the great Florentine families did the same."

"What was happening in the convent in 1630 or at the time of any of the other dates?" Charlotte asked. "Was there a particularly well-known abbess? I know very little about the history of Florence or of this convent. "

"Few people do," Isabella told her. "This convent was first opened centuries ago. When it started, it housed Dominican monks. During the time when the Medici family dominated Florence, and especially when Savonarola was the most influential religious leader, the monks here were accused of being too worldly and sinful. Eventually the pope ordered them to leave the convent and the sisters of Santa Chiara moved their congregation here. But that was in the early 1500s. I know of nothing that occurred during the dates shown on the list."

"Is there a history of the convent?" asked Charlotte eagerly. "Perhaps someone recorded the dates of important events."

Isabella stood up before she spoke, "We will go to the library and see what we can find. There should be records of important events."

The library was silent and empty when they entered. Most of the nuns were still in the chapel chanting the prayers honoring Santa Chiara's feast day. One wall of the library was filled with the manuscript copies of the earliest books in the collection. These shelves were protected by cloth curtains devoutly sewed by nuns over the years. The shelves on the other three walls held printed books bound in leather. Surely one of these would be a history of the convent.

Scanning the books was difficult for Charlotte, and even Isabella struggled. The ornate lettering on the spine of the book offered little information, so each one had to be carefully lifted down to the table and examined. Most of the volumes were devotional prayers, not the narratives the women were looking for. After half an hour of fruitless searching, they welcomed the interruption when Sister Dolorosa appeared in the doorway.

Charlotte turned eagerly toward the elderly nun. "We have been searching for a history of Santa Chiara," she said. "I would like to know more about the convent."

"Finding a history of the convent will not be easy," answered Sister Dolorosa severely. "We have devoted our time to prayers, not to glorifying the convent."

"But there have been so many pious and devoted men and women who have lived here," Isabella joined in. "Mrs. Gallagher is writing an article for a large American newspaper and would like to tell people about the work that has been done here."

The nun sat down on the wooden bench next to the library table at the center of the room. Her back was as straight as a soldier's, Charlotte noticed, although her face was deeply lined and her cheeks were hollow with age. She crossed herself silently and then began to speak.

"The convent of Santa Chiara has been a blessed place for hundreds of years. Long ago an order of monks lived here, but they, unfortunately, fell into sin and were expelled. We sisters of Santa Chiara were invited to take over the convent. We have always followed the rules of our beloved founder Santa Chiara and lived lives devoted to prayer and good works. When we enter these walls, we give up our worldly pleasures, take a new name and begin a new life. Among the women who have joined our convent are some who have come from noble families and have given up not only their jewels and titles, but also their names to become simple nuns."

Charlotte wondered whether she might find out more about some of these noble ladies, and so she asked. "The example of your convent and the lives of the nuns here must inspire many people outside the convent walls. I would like to tell my American readers something more of the lives lived here."

Sister Dolorosa pointed to the narrow panel between the window and the first bookshelf where the pictures Charlotte had noticed on her first visit were displayed. "That picture of the Madonna and the one of the angels on the opposite wall are the work of one of our nuns who lived here more than two hundred years ago. She must have been trained in painting to leave such so many accomplished works behind. There is no record of her family name. She served in the convent as Sister Opportuna. But I have heard that her family gave generous gifts to the convent and part of those gifts paid for the paints and other materials she used in her art. With the help of their gifts, she made the convent a more beautiful place for all of the nuns who worked and worshiped here."

Isabella, who had seated herself opposite Sister Dolorosa, leaned forward to ask, "Do you know of other women from wealthy families, or noble families, who have served in this convent?"

"Ah," said Sister Dolorosa, nodding her head, "It has been said that some inconvenient offspring of even the most famous Florentines have lived in this convent. I have heard that the daughter of a famous astronomer entered this convent. She sheltered here when her father was on trial for heresy. But I know nothing of her. I pray that her prayers for her father earned him a pardon for his infamous contradictions of the Bible."

"On trial for heresy! That must have been many years ago," Charlotte exclaimed.

"Yes, indeed. We are an old convent, as I told you." Sister Dolorosa leaned across the table toward Charlotte. "Will you tell the Americans about all the good works we do? Our days are passed in saying prayers for the souls of all the people of our city. We also work in the community, teaching needlework to young women, and visiting people who are sick and dying. Perhaps we will be able to gain some converts even among the protestant Americans when they hear about us. Every day I pray for unbelievers that they may be brought to the true faith."

Gradually the conversation dwindled away. Charlotte did not want to tell the elderly nun how unlikely it seemed that the convent would win many converts among Americans. But the thought of the legacy of beauty that these women, with the help of their families, had left for the city cheered her. They might have been isolated from their families and unable to live the normal life most women long for, but still they persevered in their desire to serve the community and to make art that would create some beauty in the world.

As Charlotte prepared to leave the convent to return home, she tried to imagine the long line of nuns who had served at the convent. What would have inspired one of them to leave a record of dates hidden in the chapel? What kind of secret life had been going on— perhaps was still going on—behind those ancient walls? What was life really like for these women?

Just as she was leaving, another young novice entered the library and spoke urgently to Sister Dolorosa. "Oh, Sister, we must summon a doctor. Sister Felicita is barely breathing. We have prayed as hard as we can, but she will not open her eyes. I am afraid she is dying."

CHAPTER EIGHT

Old Friends and New

Though we travel the world over to find the beautiful, we must carry it with us or we find it not.
Ralph Waldo Emerson

When Charlotte woke the next morning, she thought again about Sister Felicita and wondered whether the young nun had recovered. She and the other guests had been quickly and quietly ushered out of Santa Chiara, but surely Isabella would send news about the young woman and what the doctor had said.

It wasn't long before a brief note arrived from Isabella. *"I write to let you know that Sister Felicita was far from dying yesterday. I think perhaps it was just an hysterical attack. But what could have brought it on? A doctor was sent for and he prescribed some nasty-looking medicine. The nuns are saying extra prayers. I am hoping the mysterious troubles we have had in recent days will soon disappear."*

75

A few days later, as Charlotte walked slowly through the Piazza San Giovanni pushing Margaret Mary's perambulator, she noticed a figure walking ahead of her. It was a man, shorter and thinner than most Americans, and dressed in the dark suit and hat of a clergyman or an elderly professor. Something about the hesitant way he walked seemed familiar and when he stopped to examine a flower stall, she caught a glimpse of his face and realized he was Horace Sumner, an old friend she hadn't seen for years.

"Good morning, Mr. Sumner," she greeted him. "Do you remember me from Massachusetts? The Brook Farm Community? I met both you and your brother Charles there several years ago."

"Of course I remember you, Miss Edgerton. Could this be your own child?"

"Yes, this is Margaret Mary. And I am no longer Miss Edgerton, but Mrs. Gallagher. It is very pleasant to see a familiar face from home. Are you living in Italy now or are you a visitor?"

"I am only a visitor I am afraid, although I would dearly love to live in Florence among all this beautiful art. My brother Charles traveled to Florence several years ago and he was so impressed by the city that I determined I would follow his footsteps. May I walk with you a while?"

As they strolled around the edges of the piazza, Sumner turned to her and said, "And what of you? I believe I had heard you moved back to England where you were born."

"Yes, but my husband and I never planned to stay in England permanently. We lived there for a few years because my husband accepted a position as an editor of a newspaper in London. We intend to return to America. We are glad to see so many Americans are living in Florence now. Most of them are artists. Is that your ambition too?

"No, I fear I have no talent for art. I am an appreciative audience, but not a creator. I am hoping to collect some of the exquisite drawings of the Italian Renaissance and take them home to exhibit in Boston. Do you see the carving of an angel set in stone above the church doors over there? I found an early drawing of that angel and was able to add it to my collection."

"Are many of these drawings available for sale?" Charlotte inquired.

"A few of them are. Many families have held the paintings of the great artists like Da Vinci and Michelangelo in their collections for hundreds of years and are loathe to give them up. But the times are turbulent in Europe these days and there are some families who are in need of money and are willing to sell a few of the smaller drawings. And some monasteries have fallen upon hard times and had to sell drawings, paintings, and other art works given to them generations ago."

"Ah, I have visited Santa Chiara several times. And I have seen some of the drawings in their collection. Many of them are by Antonino Pellarosa. You would enjoy seeing the collections at Santa Chiara I am sure."

As they parted, Charlotte thanked young Sumner for his advice and urged him to call upon her and Daniel some Sunday afternoon soon. The next day she received a graceful note from him saying that he was eager to continue her acquaintance, so Charlotte was not surprised when a note from the wife of his friend, the sculptor Horatio Greenough, arrived.

On Sunday afternoons, the Greenoughs often held informal receptions where many members of the American colony gathered. Mrs. Greenough wrote to invite Charlotte to come the following Sunday and to bring her friends for tea. Charlotte was happy to accept and she invited Isabella, Marcus, and Timothy to join her and Daniel.

Almost as soon as Charlotte and her friends entered the parlor, they saw a number of familiar faces. Horatio Greenough and his wife, Louisa, welcomed them warmly and Horace Sumner came bustling over to be introduced.

Charlotte broke away from the group to greet Margaret Fuller, who was sitting in a comfortable chair near the window. She was delighted to meet Charlotte again. "Ah, I have not seen you since our brief visit in London a few years ago. I have been living in Rome and writing articles from there for Mr. Greeley's newspaper. But now that the revolutionary forces in Rome have been defeated and the Austrians have taken over the city, I have fled to Florence like so many others."

There was much to talk about, especially the surprising news that Miss Fuller had married an Italian and was now known as the Marchese Ossoli. She introduced her husband, a quiet man with the luxuriant mustache of an Italian aristocrat and the erect posture of a military officer.

Isabella was pleased to meet Margaret Fuller. Even in the convent she had heard of the famous writer and journalist. Margaret Fuller recognized Isabella's name. "Mrs. Onofrio, I remember hearing about you years ago in Boston. You are one of the Talbots, aren't you? And you married an Italian. Have you lived in Italy ever since?"

"Yes, I have lived in Florence all this time," Isabella explained. "Even though I lost my husband and my small son. I have never returned to Boston."

"The name of Pietro Onofrio was well known to me," added Signor Ossoli, "although I did not know him well. During the Napoleonic Wars and later in the 1820s, he belonged to a secret society here in Tuscany with which I had ties, the Green Brigade. I am a Roman and many of us were also filled with enthusiasm for the unification of all of Italy from Naples to Venice."

"But the revolutionaries failed in that attempt, didn't they?" Isabella remarked sadly. "The Austrians defeated them and became the rulers of northern Italy. My husband went to America and many other rebellious young people went to England and became painters or musicians. Did you go to England, Signor Ossoli?"

"No, I remained in Rome. I am not an artist nor could I be one. My training is as a soldier and my family has a long history in Rome. I did not wish to leave, although my heart wept for the dream of a united Italy.

"While I was in Rome, I wrote often to people I knew in Florence. I asked about Onofrio, but no one could ever tell me what became of him. One friend told me he thought Onofrio had died but no one seemed to know for sure. I am honored to meet you, Signora Onofrio, your husband was a credit to Florence and to Italy."

"Someday Italy will be free and united," Margaret Fuller interposed. "Just as we Americans broke away from England, so Italy will free itself from other European powers."

Charlotte tried to steer the conversation into a more cheerful direction. "Signora Onofrio has been living at the Santa Chiara convent for the past few years. I am sure the beauty of the art works there must help to restore hope for the future."

By this time Horace Sumner had joined the group. He mentioned how much he wanted to see some of the treasures of Santa Chiara. "I would like to copy some of the objects so I can take pictures of them back to America and exhibit them there. Many Americans would like to learn more about Italian art."

A few days after the meeting at the Greenoughs, Isabella arranged for Horace Sumner, to visit the convent with Charlotte to see some of the art pieces that the Onofrio family and others had given the convent. Isabella Onofrio suggested that they come early in the afternoon when the light would be good for viewing the paintings. Marcus and Timothy were glad to give up their afternoon lessons to visit Santa Chiara.

The group walked slowly through the afternoon sunlight to Santa Chiara where they stood outside for a few minutes admiring the statues in their niches on the front wall of the church before joining Isabella who was waiting for them in the parlor.

"First I will take you through the chapel and show you the altarpiece, which is a painting of the Assumption of the Virgin Mary. There is also a set of Stations of the Cross. They have been in the chapel for almost three hundred years, but alas some of them are missing. No one seems to know whether they were given away or were stolen."

As the group walked around the chapel, they admired the glowing colors of the altarpiece and the more muted tones of the four remaining pictures in the set of Stations of the Cross. "Did the Onofrio family give all of these paintings?" asked Marcus.

"There are very few records of the family's gifts to the convent. My husband spoke as though there had been many over the years," answered Isabella, "but there is no record in the convent's books about when various paintings or objects were given. My husband was quite interested in finding out more about the history of the convent and his family's connections to it." She sighed deeply. "But, of course, he had little time to investigate libraries and records."

"I am glad that the altarpiece is the one firmly associated with the Onofrios," Horace Sumner remarked. "That is a remarkable painting; the figures are so lifelike and the composition inspires reverence."

"Now I want to show you something that is a particular treasure of the convent and the most precious gift the Onofrios gave to it" Isabella told them. "It is a chalice made by one of the great goldsmiths of Florence. The abbess keeps it in a special cabinet, which is only opened once a year when the convent celebrates the feast day of Santa Chiara. Today, however, I have permission to show this treasure to you. Please take a seat and I will fetch it. "

Isabella left, but returned in a few minutes. "There has been a mistake. The chalice is missing. I must ask you to wait a little longer while I try to find out what happened to it."

When Isabella left the room, the others sat quietly in the parlor waiting expectantly. Timothy paced back and forth impatiently at one end of the room, looking up every time there was the slightest noise. "How could the nuns misplace such a valuable treasure?"

"That is what Bishop Lucca will be asking, I am afraid," responded Daniel. "He seems to have some kind of grudge against the convent. When he hears of this, I am afraid he will cause more trouble."

Charlotte jumped into the conversation to defend the nuns. "If somehow a thief has seized the chalice, it is certainly not the fault of the nuns. Other treasures have disappeared from Santa Chiara. And no doubt from other churches and monasteries too. That is not usually the fault of those who are defending the treasures. There is a great deal of crime in Florence, as there is throughout Italy. Revolutionary forces are not always careful to protect the property of aristocrats or of the church. Many of the revolutionaries are strongly opposed to the church."

When Isabella returned, she tried to reassure the others. "There must be a simple explanation," she insisted hopefully. "I am sure this is just a mistake and Abbess Josepha will explain it all soon. I apologize for not be able to show the chalice today, but we must postpone that pleasure for another day."

Isabella's face was strained and her cheer seemed forced, but she assured the visitors that the mistake would be discovered soon and the chalice found. Charlotte too smiled bravely as she led the visitors from the convent, but a sense of foreboding hung over her as they walked across the square to return to their lodgings. The sky was dark and Charlotte shivered when a sudden flash of lightning cast an eerie glow over the convent.

CHAPTER NINE

Questions and Threats

Nearly all the evils in the Church have arisen from bishops desiring power more than light.
    John Ruskin

The next morning during the quiet hour after matins prayers, Isabella walked reluctantly to the office of the abbess to ask about the precious chalice. Her steps were slow as she pondered what could have happened. Something was not right. The abbess was not a woman who made careless mistakes. She would not have forgotten her promise. Isabella could not remember a time when the chalice had been taken out of its safe storage place except for the annual celebration of Santa Chiara's feast day when the bishop said mass at the convent. Surely if the bishop or any other dignitary had asked to borrow the chalice, the abbess would have mentioned it. Such an honor would be unusual and the nuns would have celebrated the fame of their treasure.

When Isabella knocked on the door of the abbess's office, she heard no movement within. She stood in the hallway listening for a moment, but everything was quiet. At last one of the novices came down the hall, sweeping the floor carefully and looking curiously at Isabella.

"Ah, Signora Onofrio, are you looking for Abbess Josepha?" Isabella nodded. "Have you not heard that she has gone to Assisi for a retreat? She will be there for a week or more praying for peace and for the salvation of the souls of those who have forsaken the Church—may God turn their hearts back to righteousness."

Isabella thanked the novice for her information and went back to her room. She pondered whether she should wait for the abbess to return before mentioning the disappearance of the chalice. She was troubled by the thought that the abbess had apparently left the convent without telling anyone the chalice had been moved. It seemed unlikely she would do that. Could it be that the abbess did not know the chalice was missing? Would she blame Isabella for somehow losing the chalice or misplacing it?

That night Isabella had trouble sleeping. She woke several times wondering why she felt so uneasy. Despite her confidence in telling Charlotte and the others that the abbess would solve the mystery, she felt far less certain herself. Only a few days ago the chalice had been used in the saint's day mass. Perhaps a thief had invaded the convent and somehow found the hiding place where the chalice was kept. Who would know where that was? Even the novices did not know. Only a few trusted nuns and Isabella herself. And why would a nun take the chalice? What could she do with it if she had it?

The long night continued as Isabella tossed and turned. What would the abbess do now? If she had been the abbess, who would she have turned to if she discovered a theft in the convent? Of course the answer was—the bishop. He must be notified if there was any chance such a valuable chalice had been stolen. Yes, she must tell the bishop. She would call on him and tell him what had happened. Once she had decided, she was able to fall deeply asleep.

When she woke the next morning, Isabella was disappointed to see rain coming down outside her window. But she had made up her mind and she would go to the bishop's palace despite the weather. It would be unseemly for her to go alone, so she asked one of the young novices to come with her. Together they walked across the wet, slippery streets until they faced the impressive marble façade of the bishop's palace. Resolutely Isabella led the way up the steps.

When a young priest answered the door, Isabella explained who she was and why she had requested an audience with the bishop. She and the novice, Sister Angela, waited in the elaborate hallway while the priest disappeared in the further reaches of the luxurious building.

Finally the monk returned and beckoned them to follow him. He led the way through a long passage hung with portraits of previous bishops of Florence. Each one was set in a gold frame and lighted with a votive candle. Even though it was daylight outside, the candles were lit and Isabella caught glimpses of the stern faces of the bishops. As the faces followed her down the hall, she felt insignificant and much younger than she had felt for many years.

At last the priest brought them into a small dark study. Shelves filled with leather-bound books lined the walls and a large walnut table filled the center of the room. Two windows let in the gloomy light of the rainy day and a candelabra filled with lighted candles was set on the desk. Behind the flickering candles sat the bishop in his red-trimmed cassock, his face half obscured by the shadowy light. He smiled when he saw the two women.

"What is it you want, my daughters? I understand you come from the convent of Santa Chiara with urgent news for me."

"Your Excellency, I am troubled by a discovery that I made yesterday at the convent," Isabella began. "The Abbess Josepha gave me permission to show our most valuable chalice to some guests from America. When I opened the cabinet where it is kept, I discovered the chalice was not there. I immediately went to tell the abbess, of course, but she has left to attend a retreat in Assisi this week. Perhaps there is some reason why the chalice has been removed from its customary place, but I was worried about it, so I thought I ought to tell you."

"You did well to come to me" The bishop's frown, lit by the flickering candles made him look angry, but his voice was calm. "I know nothing about this. The chalice has certainly not been removed at my request. Perhaps Abbess Josepha had a reason to take it from its usual place, although it seems strange she did not tell you if she did. But I will ask one of the priests to investigate the matter. You can say a special prayer today to ask Our Lady to restore the chalice to its rightful place. Your story troubles me."

The bishop leaned forward on the table, his heavy brows creased into a frown. "Perhaps taking care of valuable sacred objects is too heavy a task for women. When the abbess returns, I will speak to her again about the changes we have been discussing these past few months. I am beginning to believe it may be God's will that the convent should be returned to the Dominican monks who lived there in the past. They have had many years to repent the sins that led to their dismissal. Every year Florence becomes a larger and more important city attracting visitors from many countries. It is not fitting that a quiet group of nuns should be in charge of one of the city's most important convents. A group of strong monks would be better able to protect the convent's art works. Go my children and do not trouble yourself further. I will take care of this matter."

Isabella leaned forward to speak again, but the bishop waved his hand to signal that the conversation was over. The young priest led them to the door. Once more they walked down the long hallway lined with the pictures of long-dead bishops. The reception room through which they had entered now held quite a large group of people waiting to see the bishop. There were two army officers in elaborate uniforms, a trio of monks in long black robes, and several richly dressed merchants.

By the time Isabella and the young nun left the building, the rain had stopped and the sun was rapidly drying the cobblestones of the street, but storm clouds were gathering within Isabella. The bishop seemed to blame the nuns for the loss of the chalice. He had spoken to her and Sister Angela as if they were children. Isabella, who even after many years in Italy was not quite accustomed to the autocratic behavior of priests and especially bishops, was not pleased to be treated as though she had no role to play in finding out what had happened. After all, the chalice was part of her husband's legacy to the convent. She felt she had the right to be involved in keeping it safe.

Instead of going back to the convent, she turned to Sister Angela. "Come. We will call on my American friends before returning. The sun has come out and the director of novices will not object to your staying out a little longer. She knows you are safe with me."

They found Charlotte sitting on the balcony of her lodging house watching Margaret Mary as she contentedly arranged her three dolls on a chair and tried to feed them petals from the bougainvillea flowers that trailed over the railing.

After listening to the account of the visit, she asked "Why do you think the bishop told you nothing more than to stop worrying and let him take care of the problem? Is he really going to use this as an excuse to give the convent to the monks?" Charlotte was almost as disturbed by that idea as Isabella was.

Isabella answered slowly. "The bishop believes that no woman should trouble herself about anything serious. Except perhaps for the abbess, who has some power. But the bishop looks upon me as just the widow of a man who has left no heirs. He does not think he has to take me into account. But I am determined that my husband's family and its legacy will be guarded and honored as it should be. He is no longer alive to protect his family so I believe I should take on his duties. The chalice belongs to the convent, but it is a reminder that the Onofrio family was an important and honorable family in Florence and should not be forgotten. If the chalice is lost forever, much of their legacy will disappear."

"Do you really think someone might have stolen the chalice?" Charlotte asked. "Even though it is a beautiful and valuable object, no thief could sell it because it would be recognized. You do not think anyone would melt it down, do you? That would take away much of its value."

"It could be sold to a visitor to this city," Isabella reminded her. "Wealthy men from England and America often buy Italian art objects to add to their collections. As Italians become poorer, they have been forced to sell many of their treasures overseas."

No matter how long they talked, there was nothing they could think of doing that would restore the chalice to its place. Isabella said she would consult the abbess as soon as she returned from her retreat in Assisi. She also had one more idea.

"Charlotte, you have told me that you and your husband were able to solve several mysterious crimes both in New York and in London. Would you be willing to help me solve this strange mystery here in Florence?"

Charlotte was eager to help her new friend, although she confessed that it would be difficult to find a way of doing that. She and Daniel were strangers in the city and knew very little about its laws and customs. But Isabella was persistent and insisted that someone new to the city might see things with a fresh eye and shed light on the motives of people involved with the convent. The two women talked for almost an hour before Isabella and the young nun left.

CHAPTER TEN

A Difficult Search

The desire of gold is not for gold. It is for the means of freedom and benefit.
Ralph Waldo Emerson

After Isabella left, Charlotte paced back and forth in her parlor trying to devise a plan for investigating the disappearance of the chalice. Finally she decided that her first step would be another visit to the convent. There must be more clues to be found in the history of the building and the various families who had supported it over the years. Perhaps she could find out why the bishop seemed so indifferent to the loss of the chalice and why he was so determined to allow the monks to return. Her request for permission to see Sister Dolorosa was granted, and the two women sat on a bench in the cloister to talk.

"I would like to know more about the chalice the Onofrio family gave to the convent many years ago," Charlotte explained. "The one we had hoped to see yesterday. I have been told it is the greatest treasure of Santa Chiara. What is it that makes it so special? Was it made by a famous artist?"

Sister Dolorosa was silent for a moment as she contemplated the full-blooms of the white roses on the bush in front of their bench. One petal detached itself in the gentle wind and wafted slowly to the grass below. Finally the nun spoke.

"I do not know whether the artist was famous. It was made by a goldsmith here in Florence. It is the story of the chalice that makes it such a special and valuable gift to the convent. Many years ago, the Onofrio family were rich and powerful bankers in the city. Like most powerful men, the head of the family was a soldier who fought for the Grand Duke of Tuscany. And his sons were also warriors in those long wars that were fought against the barbarians and infidels of the East."

The nun sighed and turned her head away for a moment, then continued. "They were brave soldiers and the family flourished. But as the years wore on, bad luck fell upon them. Their children died young, or died in childbirth. Sons went on crusades and never came back. Some of their ships sank while they were bringing spices back from the East.

"By 1547, the family was much smaller and much poorer than it had been. The head of the family, Alessandro Onofrio, was counting on his son, Cosimo, to revive the family fortunes. Cosimo had gone to the Indies to bring back a cargo of precious spices. He would take them to Naples to sell and then bring the gold to Florence. But before reaching Naples, Cosimo's ship was attacked by pirates from Sardinia. A few of the sailors escaped by jumping overboard and swimming to shore, but most perished. Cosimo fought bravely, but he was killed along with many of his men. The pirates took their prizes from the ship and left it drifting in the sea, with Captain Onofrio's body tied to the wheel."

The horror of a ship captained by the dead man, chilled Charlotte as she listened. "What did his father do when he heard the news?"

"Alessandro was in despair for weeks after the death of his son. But Cosimo Onofrio's wife was expecting a child and Alessandro put his hopes into the child. He commissioned the chalice, solid gold decorated with diamonds and rubies, as a reminder of the blood shed by his son. Alessandro prayed to God that his grandson would redeem the honor of the family.

"And his prayers were answered. His grandson grew up to be a great warrior who adopted a new coat of arms for the Onofrios. Solid black with a red cross in the middle. The grandson was called the Black Warrior and year-by-year he retrieved the fortunes of the family. Alessandro donated the chalice to our convent in gratitude and we have had it ever since. In every generation of the Onofrio family there has been a Black Warrior who has kept the family from disappearing. Some have said that young Pietro Onofrio was a Black

Warrior but he went to America and came back with a foreign wife. Some people say that was a betrayal of the family, that he should have married a Florentine who would have bred sons worthy of the city. And when Pietro returned from America and joined the fight for democracy again, he did not become the hero his family had hoped for. Instead, he mysteriously disappeared. His companions were disappointed. Many of them became bitter and dispirited. And not long after that, the Austrians seemed to gain strength and the revolution failed again."

"But Pietro Onofrio was killed, wasn't he? His wife told me he was a hero."

"Ah, perhaps he was killed. But I have heard it whispered that he did not die but instead fled from the battle and betrayed his city. No one knows the truth except the good God above us."

The old nun's voice was getting weaker and Charlotte could see that she was tiring. There were more questions to be asked, but Charlotte decided to wait until another day. It seemed kinder to say good-by to Sister Dolorosa and walk home. The afternoon was already growing dark and Daniel would be waiting for her.

Early the following morning, Charlotte sat down at a small table in the parlor to write the details of the history Sister Dolorosa had told her. She would have to talk to Isabella about the nun's story, although she was afraid it might disturb her new friend. She did not look forward to discussing the matter.

A few minutes later she was surprised by a caller. Isabella burst into speech almost as soon as she had said hello.

"The loss of the chalice will bring even greater trouble than I had feared," she announced. "Yesterday the bishop told me that the convent has been careless. You know he has talked to Abbess Josepha about allowing the monks to take over Santa Chiara. I had not thought this plan was truly serious, but it seems the bishop is eager. Today a message from the bishop's office requests a meeting with Abbess Josepha as soon as she returns from Assisi."

"We must find out more about this," Charlotte said. "Did your husband often speak to you about that chalice and about his family's history?"

"My husband was a modern man. It is true that he was called the Black Warrior when he was fighting the Austrians for the freedom of Florence. That was a traditional name in the family, and I think he liked having it, but he never took the old superstitions very seriously. He honored his family's history, but he believed that people must build their own lives here on earth and not expect God to send miracles to help them. He scorned superstitious people who insisted on lucky pieces and charms to help them."

"I suppose whoever took the chalice felt the same. It was not its symbolic value, but the practical value of the gold and gems that attracted the thief," Charlotte said thoughtfully.

"Yes," agreed Isabella, "and it is important that we try to find out where the chalice is and who took it before the abbess returns. She will be outraged when she learns it has disappeared. And especially when she has heard what the bishop said."

"Was the chalice last used on the feast day of Santa Chiara? That was not long ago."

"Yes, you and I both saw it on that day. That is when the bishop came to celebrate mass at the convent. After that it would have been returned to the cabinet," Isabella responded.

"That narrows the time down," Charlotte was quick to point out. "Perhaps we can look at the guest book to see who has visited the library since the feast day."

"Yes," replied Isabella slowly. "Of course, not everyone signs the guest book. People can visit the cloister at will and sometimes they stop in the chapel or library for an informal visit. But visitors who request permission to use the library are asked to sign the book. Perhaps you and your husband could find out who our recent visitors have been."

Later that afternoon, while Margaret Mary napped under the watchful eye of Maria Spinelli, Charlotte and Daniel made their way to the convent. When they knocked at the door of the private area, they asked for Signora Onofrio. While the novice went off to look for her, Daniel walked over to examine the guestbook

DEATH ENTERS THE CONVENT | 101

lying on a sturdy oak table at the side of the room. He took out his familiar reporter's pad and his pencil and quickly copied as many names as he could decipher. The names were signed in ornate, swirling letters that were difficult to read, but fortunately there were not many of them.

Isabella soon joined them and the three of them were able to make a list of the recent visitors. It was easy to recognize the name of Bishop Lucca. A name below his was deciphered by Isabella as Father Carlucci, one of the bishop's assistants. They also found the names of Lorenzo Tanassi and Giovanni Bagnoli, Timothy's art teacher. There were four or five other names that Daniel carefully copied, although he did not recognize any of them.

Daniel led the group out into the cloister where they sat on a shady bench and studied the notebook. Isabella was able to identify two of the unfamiliar names as those of the parents of two of the nuns. They had no doubt visited to see their daughters and perhaps give a gift to the convent. The third unknown name was written in what looked like a foreign script. Daniel had tried to puzzle out the letters, but was not certain about them.

"I am not sure this list gets us any closer to the solution of the mystery," Daniel said. "It seems unlikely that the parents or relatives of any nun at the convent would be responsible. And certainly the bishop and his secretary could not be suspected of such behavior."

"That leaves only Signor Tanassi and Signor Bagnoli, both of whom we know and neither of whom has ever been suspected of any theft or crime. They are above reproach as much as the bishop and his secretary, I should think." Charlotte was disappointed. "Do you suppose someone got into the convent in another way and found the hiding place?"

Isabella sounded discouraged as she agreed. "A stranger in the convent would be noticed, I think, unless they just stayed in the cloister. When the abbess comes back, I can ask her about other visitors, but I hope we can find out more about the chalice before that happens."

The afternoon's investigation had not yielded much, so as Charlotte and Daniel walked back to their lodgings, they talked about what could come next.

"If someone stole the chalice to melt it down," Charlotte asked. "Where would he take it? Who would actually melt it and make the gold into coins or something that can be sold? I know nothing about how this is done."

"No more do I," Daniel confessed. "Who would be able to tell us about this?"

"A goldsmith, I suppose." Charlotte suggested. "Why don't I visit a goldsmith and see whether I can learn anything?"

The next day she did just that. She took Maria
Spinelli and Margaret Mary with her so she could pose
as a woman looking for gold ornaments or something
for her husband. Together they walked through the
narrow, twisting streets. The cobblestones were
difficult to navigate and Margaret Mary often needed to
be carried, but they soon came to the neighborhood
where many shops had the traditional signs of the
goldsmith trade.

Charlotte had to lower her head as she stepped into
one of the first shops on the street. An elderly man
wearing a green smock bent over a table on which were
spread several gold chains and coins as well as a small
scale for weighing coins. "Can I help you, signora?" he
asked.

"My husband has inherited a number of old gold
rings and bracelets from his grandmother and we are
considering having them melted down and made into
something else," explained Charlotte. "Do you do that
sort of work?"

"I would have to see the chains and gold pieces that
you have. Some gold has been adulterated with baser
metals and is not easy to work with. Melting gold is not
an easy task and unless you have a great many rings
and bracelets, they would not be worth wasting time
on. What do you want to have made from them?"

"That depends on how much gold there actually is in
the collection. I had hoped to make a chalice or other
religious vessel for presentation to our church. It would

be in honor of my mother. God rest her soul! Do you have any experience working with such vessels?"

"Wait here a moment, Signora, and I will show you some of the things we have done." The man called out to someone in the back of the shop and gave orders in Italian spoken so quickly that Charlotte could not make out what he was saying. A few minutes later a tall, husky young man with black hair sweeping down over his forehead and a leather apron encasing much of his body came out carrying two gold objects. He placed them on the counter.

"Here are some examples of the work we do," the goldsmith announced. "These are some of our recent commissions." Picking up one, he explained "This is a monstrance we made for the pastor of the Church of Our Lady of Sorrows. See how it gleams and how the delicately wrought tracery around the edge show the depth and color of the gold." He smiled at it proudly before turning to the other object.

"This," he said, holding it up, "is the chalice we made for the Monastery of the Holy Cross. As you can see, it is very plain, in accordance with the wishes of the holy monks, but the single amethyst brightens it up and makes it very special."

"Have you worked on other chalices?" asked Charlotte. "Have you ever seen the chalice at the convent of Santa Chiara? The one that was given to them by the Onofrio family? I have heard it is the most beautiful chalice in Florence."

"Oh, it is hardly that!" the goldsmith protested. "I have heard that it is lovely, but there are many other chalices in Florence that surpass it. And I say proudly that my father and grandfather have worked on the handsomest chalices in the city."

Charlotte hesitated before she asked the next question. "If a church, or a monastery needed money, would they ask a goldsmith to melt down a chalice and make it into something that could be sold?"

"What are you suggesting?" asked the goldsmith, suddenly frowning and peering at her suspiciously. "Surely no priest or monk would destroy a sacred vessel to make trinkets. You told me you were interested in melting old jewelry, not church vessels. What are you thinking?"

"Oh, no! I would not dream of melting down a vessel that had been blessed for a church, nor would my husband," Charlotte insisted. "But I have heard of such things being done. And recently I have heard that some church vessels have been stolen—not here, but in Rome," Charlotte flushed with embarrassment as she made up the story. "I was just wondering what a thief who stole such a sacred vessel would think of doing with it."

"There is no doubt a villain like that could find a dishonest goldsmith to melt down a stolen vessel and turn it into coins or jewelry that could be sold for gain. But you will not find such thieves in this city. The Goldsmith Guild vouches for the honesty of all its members. Anyone who deals in stolen goods is cast out of the Guild. I have heard that in large cities such as Rome, or perhaps Naples, such people congregate and have a trade in stolen objects, but I do not think you would find such people in Florence, or indeed in all of Tuscany."

Charlotte decided she had learned all that she could from the goldsmith. Besides, Margaret Mary was becoming restless and needed to be taken home for her nap. Promising to return with her husband as soon as she had the chance, Charlotte left the shop and headed back to the lodging house.

CHAPTER ELEVEN

Troubling Questions

Suspicion is the cancer of friendship.
Petrarch

Shortly after Santa Chiara's feast day, came the rituals of Easter Week, which brought all of Florence to a standstill. The Palm Sunday procession of priests and nuns carrying green branches gave way to the somber penitential hymns of Good Friday and those were followed by the lavish choral outbursts of Easter Sunday. Timothy sighed with impatience as he waited for something to happen. His studies continued to go well. Marcus was satisfied with his essays and translations and Signor Bagnoli praised his drawings. Day after day in Signor Bagnoli's studio, the students devoted themselves to drawing careful pictures of the bowls of fruit or flowers given to them as models, or to copying drawings that other artists had made of buildings and scenery.

One morning Timothy grumbled to one of the other boys, "I am tired of copying fruit and flowers. Do you suppose we will ever be allowed to draw pictures of people?"

Signor Bagnoli overheard him, and frowned at Timothy. "Do you think you are ready to draw from live models, young man?"

"No, I know I need to work more to reach that level. But I know that some of the great artists have left collections of drawings of real people that we could use as models. I have seen some in the churches here. Leonardo Da Vinci is well known for his drawings from life. Perhaps we could get permission to copy some of those."

"Where have you seen these marvelous drawings?"

"I have met a woman who lives in the Santa Chiara Convent. She is a relative of my tutor and she showed us some of the collections there."

Signor Bagnoli frowned deeply. "And who is this woman?"

"Signora Onofrio. Her husband was a patriot." Timothy was startled at the look that came over his teacher's face when he said that. Instead of smiling at the name, Bagnoli appeared troubled. He frowned deeply and turned away from Timothy.

"There is little you can believe and few people you can trust in this city. I would not pay attention to anything such a woman says. You will learn to draw by doing as I say and copying the models here."

Timothy was surprised by Signor Bagnoli's reaction, but he said nothing and returned to his copying. He noticed some of the other students looking at him and finally one of them, Enrico, leaned over and whispered, "Signora Onofrio is the widow of a traitor, not a hero. Pietro Onofrio tried to destroy the Tuscan Republic. He betrayed his comrades to the Austrians and ran away. Do not be too friendly to that woman."

Even though Timothy's Italian was still limited, he understood every word Enrico said. He struggled to answer. "I can't believe that is true. Signora Onofrio lost her husband and her son. She said her husband was a revolutionary. Why would she tell lies?"

Enrico shrugged. "She is not a Florentine. Maybe she sympathizes with the Austrians. My father says that Pietro Onofrio was once an honored rebel leader, but he suddenly disappeared. While others were still fighting, he did not help them. Soon after the Austrians attacked again and the rebels were defeated. Someone betrayed the rebels. It must have been Onofrio."

Enrico turned back to his work, but his scornful glances told Timothy that the boy agreed with Signor Bagnoli. It seemed that the enemies of Pietro Onofrio were strong and certain of what they said.

When Timothy got home, he questioned Marcus. "Signor Bagnoli and some of the boys in my art class say that Signora Onofrio is not to be trusted. They say her husband was a traitor."

"That's not possible," Marcus frowned as he spoke. "Why would she lie when she tells us about her husband? I do not believe my aunt would marry a traitor. I do not want to hear her spoken of as if she had done something wrong."

Timothy said nothing more about what he had heard during his drawing class, but later that day when he and Marcus called on Charlotte, he was glad to see Isabella was also there. He watched her as they listened to Charlotte's account of her visit to the goldsmith.

"It seems unlikely that the chalice would be stolen for the value of its gold," Isabella argued. "Even though the jewels set into the gold are also valuable, the piece as a whole is of far greater value than the price of the materials that made it."

"Yes," Daniel added thoughtfully. "But if the chalice were taken out of Florence, it could be sold to a connoisseur who valued such magnificent art and would not know it had been stolen."

"Do you think someone who signed the guestbook at the convent could have stolen it?" Timothy was impatient to take some action.

"The only two names we recognized on the list were those of Signor Bagnoli and Signor Tanassi," Charlotte reminded him. "Both of those gentlemen are highly respectable. How could we even question them?"

"Sometimes very respectable people do wicked things," insisted Timothy. He was thinking about what Signor Bagnoli had told him. If Marcus's aunt could be a traitor, then anyone could be suspect.

"Are we sure they are so respectable?" he asked. "What do we really know about Signor Tanassi after all? He took care of Marcus, but he admitted his paintings were not selling well. Perhaps he needs money."

Isabella shook her head impatiently. "I do not see how we could possibly question Signor Tanassi about this. He would be insulted."

No one else had a suggestion, and conversation languished. When Isabella declared she would go back to Santa Chiara to be there for vespers, Marcus volunteered to walk with her to the convent.

"But you had better go back home to work on the Latin translation," he warned Timothy.

As Timothy walked along the cobblestone street toward the lodging house, he scowled, thinking how much he would like to solve the mystery of the theft of the chalice. No one took his ideas seriously, but if he could locate the chalice and return it to the convent, he would be a hero. As he walked past the stable where coach horses were kept, he noticed a familiar figure waiting with a group of travelers. He almost called out loud as he recognized the man was Lorenzo Tanassi. He was carrying a large carpetbag and talking seriously with the coach driver.

Timothy walked around the coach, so Lorenzo could not see him. He noticed a boy, about his age, loading baggage onto the top of the coach and called to him. "Where is this coach going?"

"To Pisa."

Impulsively Timothy jumped up beside the boy. "Let me ride on top. I have to visit my grandmother. She's dying."

The boy smiled knowingly at his broken Italian. "Dying, eh? And you have no money?"

"I don't have enough for the coach. I'll give you a *scudo* if you let me sit up here."

"Show me your money. But don't let the driver see it." Once the coin was safely stored in the boy's pocket, he extended his hand to help Timothy climb up beside him and settle in half-hidden by the shabby luggage piled up behind them.

The driver cracked his whip and the heavily laden coach rumbled off. Although the road was rough the coach moved steadily forward. Four horses strained toward the sun sinking slowly into the horizon in front of them. As the boy beside him started singing softly, Timothy leaned back and felt that at last he was doing something worthwhile. The hooves of the horses pounded rhythmically on the dusty road and Timothy had to clench his fists to keep from dozing off.

The sun was below the horizon and daylight was fading when the towers of Pisa appeared in the distance. The horses strained harder to gain speed as they sensed their stalls were not far off. Slowly the coach rolled into the city.

"Here's the stable," the coach boy said. "Jump off fast so no one sees you." He muttered as the coach pulled up outside a shabby courtyard.

Timothy jumped down and stood in the shadow of the stable as he watched the passengers scramble out of the coach. Bags were tossed down quickly. Lorenzo Tanassi grabbed his carpetbag and strode away. He did not hesitate but seemed to know exactly where he was going.

As Tanassi turned down a narrow street, Timothy followed. Darkness was falling and silent houses loomed above them. Suddenly the street opened into a piazza. Tanassi knocked at the door of a large stone house. A sudden flash of light as the door was opened and he was quickly admitted. Now Timothy knew where he had gone, but how could he find out what he was doing? Perhaps this was just another crazy chase like the one he had led Daniel on when they were looking for Marcus.

###

Back in Florence, Elsie was worried. Soon the doors to their building would be locked and neither Timothy nor Marcus were home. They had never been this late before. She clucked to herself, "Why did I ever agree to come to this wicked, foreign city? Young gentlemen don't disappear in Boston."

Her thought was interrupted by the opening of a door as Marcus appeared. Elsie turned to him. "Where is Master Timothy? What have you two been up to?"

Marcus began pacing back and forth between the window and the door. "When I left Timothy, he was caught up in the mystery about the chalice. Could he have decided to try to solve that on his own? He heard a story about my aunt today and seems to think he can trust no one in Florence."

"Perhaps Mr. Gallagher can help you find him," Elsie suggested.

Marcus bristled at the thought. "I do not need to bother the Gallaghers. I will find him on my own. Don't worry about dinner. I will have something when I get back."

The streets were fully dark now, but Marcus was able to borrow a lantern from the *patrone* who guarded the door. He turned to walk toward Santa Chiara to speak to his aunt, but slowed down after a few steps. The convent doors were probably closed and locked for the night. He would have to wait until morning No, he would ask Signor Tanassi. Wasn't that what Timothy had suggested? He turned resolutely and hurried toward the Tanassi palazzo.

The large gates to the palazzo were closed when Marcus arrived, and the house lay dark and silent under the fitful light of a crescent moon. Marcus knocked on the wooden gate but got no response. He pounded heavily making as much noise as he could, but heard nothing. As he stood outside the gate panting after his exertions trying to decide what to do next, he finally heard a stirring inside the gate.

A voice called "*Chi va là?*"

Marcus recognized the voice of Alfredo, the Tanassi's doorman, and responded loudly, "It is I, Marcus Talbot".

Slowly the gate opened enough to let the man inside peer into the street and recognize Marcus. In his broken Italian Marcus asked whether he could talk to Lorenzo, but was told that Signor Tanassi was away. And Signora Rizzo would surely not be accepting visitors at this hour. Still the man did not slam the gate closed, but stood smiling at Marcus.

Frowning at his lack of success, Marcus realized what was needed. He pulled out a few *scudi* and handed them to the man. "I am must reach Signor Tanassi as soon as possible. Can you tell me where he has gone?"

"Ah yes," the man nodded. "I know you are a friend of Signor Tanassi. He will want to see you, but he has gone to Signora Rizzo's palazzo in Pisa. He often takes the coach to Pisa."

After Marcus had obtained information about where the house was located, he walked slowly homeward hoping he was right in guessing that Timothy had followed Lorenzo to Pisa.

CHAPTER TWELVE

Dangerous Territory

The world has come to such a state that one can no longer find anyone who does good.
Savonarola

Marcus slept very little that night and was up at dawn to catch the morning coach to Pisa. He told Elsie where he was going and left two notes—one to be delivered to his aunt at Santa Chiara, and the other to the Gallaghers. Even though he wrote the notes quickly, he was careful to include the location of Signora Rizzo's palazzo. He shivered with anticipation as he walked through the quiet morning streets to the coach stable. Had he guessed right about Timothy?

Alternately dozing and staring out the window at the vineyards that lined the road, Marcus fretted about whether he would arrive in time to prevent Timothy from doing anything rash. When the coach pulled up at the Pisa stop, he was the first passenger to jump to the ground. He was soon at the piazza and facing the house Alfredo had described to him, but the blank stone walls offered no clue as to where Timothy could be.

Marcus walked slowly around the piazza, scanning each building he passed. The square was dominated by a church and the sounds of church bells rang out loudly. Where would Timothy have gone if he had followed Lorenzo here? Had he accosted Signor Tanassi and accused him of taking the chalice? Surely Timothy would not be so rash. Could he have found a welcome in Signora Rizzo's house? That seemed unlikely. What excuse would he give for being there? But where else could he have gone? Two elderly beggar women were sitting on the paving stones outside the church. Other shabbily dressed people were huddled close to the church walls too, but Marcus saw no familiar figure. He walked up the wide steps into the dim church and moved slowly around the walls looking into every nook and chapel.

At last he found Timothy slumped in a pew in a dark corner of the church near the confessional. The boy's eyes snapped open when Marcus shook his shoulder. "What are you doing here? How did you find me?" he asked as he rubbed his eyes.

"Just a guess. You talked so much about not trusting anyone. When I found out Lorenzo Tanassi was on his way to Pisa, I figured you might follow him. Did you learn anything?"

"Only the house where he stays. I saw him go in last night, but decided to wait until today to try to talk to him."

"*Silenzio*" hissed a black-clad woman in the pew behind them.

With a jerk on his arm, Marcus led Timothy outside to the piazza. "Have you eaten? Let's get something at that café across the square."

The café was almost as dim as the church had been. Marcus led the way to a table in the corner and they quickly ordered rolls and coffee. Timothy's unwashed face and wrinkled clothes made him look at home in the dingy workingman's café. He seized the rolls as soon as they arrived and gobbled down his share.

"Eat them all," Marcus said genially. "I'll order more." He walked toward the waiter who had served them and then stopped as he noticed a familiar figure. Lorenzo Tanassi was sitting at a small table in the corner with another man. They leaned toward each other, their heads close together and Lorenzo jabbed his finger on the table as if he were arguing.

Marcus turned toward the counter and pretended to study the brioche. A few Italian words drifted toward him as the two men talked. "*Oro…vendere…*Santa Chiara." Marcus returned quickly to Timothy.

"They are certainly talking about selling something," he told the boy. "And about Santa Chiara. He said something about that. It must be about the chalice." Marcus was trying to keep his voice down despite his excitement.

"I'm sure he had the chalice with him when he took the coach," Timothy said. "His bag was just the right size and he kept it close to him—not on top of the carriage where other baggage was stored. But how can we get it?"

"He's not carrying it now," Marcus said. "It must be in the house where he is staying. That is Signora Rizzo's house, although she is still in Florence."

"They are leaving," Timothy whispered, looking toward the door. Lorenzo and his companion stood for a few minutes in front of the café entrance, talking and gesticulating to one another before they walked off together.

"They are not going back to the house. They are going in the opposite direction," Marcus pointed out.

"Let's go to his house," Timothy suggested. "We can say we have to deliver a letter or something and get into the house. Maybe we can find the chalice and take it back to Santa Chiara. He has no right to it."

Before Marcus could reply, Timothy was out of his chair and close to the door of the café, carrying the last brioche in his hand. Marcus trailed behind, protesting weakly. "What are you going to say…?"

By this time Timothy was wiping the last of the crumbs off his hand and reaching for the bell at the entrance to the palazzo. After several rings, a servant slowly pulled the gate open. Timothy told the man they were delivering a message for Signor Tanassi. When told that Signor Tanassi was not available, Timothy immediately asked whether they could wait for him. The servant frowned at him suspiciously, but said he could wait in the courtyard until Signor Tanassi returned. He then turned and made his halting way back inside the house, bolting the door behind him as he entered.

"This doesn't get us very far," Marcus complained. "Signor Tanassi may be gone for hours."

"But look, there are windows around the courtyard. Perhaps we can see what is going on in some of these rooms. Maybe we can find another servant who will let us look inside the house. How much money do you have with you?" Excitement made Timothy's voice rise.

The narrow windows facing onto the courtyard had crude glass panels discolored by years of sun and rain. The rooms Marcus and Timothy could see through the glass looked like storerooms. In one, bulky hams hung from the beams; in another, barrels lined the walls. But then Timothy stopped at a third window and stared fixedly inside. This room had a carpet on the floor, and shelves around the walls held books and objects indistinguishable in the dim light.

As Marcus joined Timothy at the window, a shaft of sunlight illuminated one shelf which held several pictures. Timothy gasped. "Those look like the stations of the cross from Santa Chiara. They are exact copies."

"Are you sure?"

"Yes, I have looked often enough at that set of pictures. I recognize the style. Signor Bagnoli has taught us to examine everything very carefully. They were painted in a very distinctive style and are unlike any other set of the stations of the cross. That is what Signor Bagnoli told us. Why are there copies of them here in Pisa and what is Signor Tanassi planning to do with them?"

"You really have studied those pictures," Marcus admitted. He stood still for a moment and then took Timothy by the arm and pulled him toward the gate. "We must get out of here. We can't confront Tanassi on our own. Neither of us can prove that he made those copies. Perhaps he had no intention of selling them. Was he going to pretend they are originals? Or have the originals been stolen and replaced by copies?"

Marcus looked discouraged. "And there is no sign of the stolen chalice. There is something wrong about what Signor Tanassi is doing, but I'm not sure that he is a thief. We must go back to Florence to tell my aunt about this. She can inform the abbess or the bishop about what we have discovered."

"Maybe we could sneak in and steal the pictures whether they are copies or originals. We could take them to Santa Ciara ourselves and show them what is being done," Timothy urged. "Then we'd really be heroes."

"We'd be thieves. Who would believe our story? Come on, we have to get out of here."

The two of them walked back to the gate and let themselves out. Despite the shriek of the rusty hinges, no servant appeared to challenge their leaving. They turned away from the church and walked briskly toward the far end of the piazza. As Timothy turned back to look again at the palazzo, he noticed a familiar figure striding toward the gate. Was that Lorenzo? The man stood for a moment at the gate and looked toward Marcus and Timothy, or was he only looking at the noisy wagon full of poultry that was entering the square? Timothy couldn't tell for sure and when he looked back, the figure had disappeared.

The trip back to Florence was slow and tiring. Marcus's supply of money was running low, but they managed to persuade a farmer to let them go back in his wagon in return for help in loading the wagon with poultry bought in Pisa. He asked only two *scudi* for payment. Even the crates of noisy chickens couldn't keep Timothy from falling asleep as they jounced along in the heavy wooden wagon.

The wagon rumbled along much more slowly than the coach, so the sun was low in the Western sky when they arrived at the edge of Florence. The farmer dropped them off close to the river on the outskirts of the city and Marcus and Timothy trudged slowly back to their lodging. When they arrived, they found both

Charlotte and Isabella talking with Elsie about what
had happened.

"Thank heavens you found Timothy," Charlotte
exclaimed. "You both look tired and dirty. What
happened?"

Soon they were all seated around the table eating
Elsie's delicious bread and drinking tea. Timothy told
the story of how he had impulsively followed Lorenzo
to Pisa and found himself spending the night huddled
outside a church. Marcus added details about his trip
and what the two of them had seen.

"What about the chalice?" Isabella asked.

"There was no sign of that," Marcus admitted.
"Although Timothy thought Signor Tanassi might have
been carrying it on the coach. Do you suppose he has
that hidden in Pisa?"

"The house in Pisa is Signora Rizzo's home,"
Marcus added. "Alfredo told me Lorenzo Tanassi was
visiting there. He takes care of the house when Signora
Rizzo makes a long visit to Florence. They do not want
to leave the house unsupervised."

"I should think not," Timothy added. "Not when
they are hiding so many valuable art works there."

"But how can we get them back? We must tell the
abbess about this," Charlotte said.

"How many pictures are there in the storeroom?"
Isabella asked. "I wonder whether they are all from
Santa Chiara. Can we get any description of them?"

"I can draw some of them. I was able to see them through the window although the light was not good," Timothy answered. "You can show the pictures to Abbess Josepha. She will probably recognize the ones from Santa Chiara."

Timothy spent the next day laboring over his drawings. Although he could not remember every detail of the three paintings he had seen, his quick eye had caught the general outline of each picture and the figures in them. He and Marcus took the drawings to Santa Chiara and gave them to Isabella.

"This happened just in time," Isabella told them. "The abbess has returned from her retreat, so I will show these to her today. She may want to speak to the two of you and hear more about where these were found."

"We will be ready to speak with her whenever she is ready," Marcus replied, while Timothy beamed with pride. At last he had done something he could really be proud of. But as he turned away from the others, he had to admit to himself that he was disappointed he had not found the chalice.

CHAPTER THIRTEEN

Disappointments

The best laid schemes of mice and men, go often askew.
Robert Burns

As soon as morning coffee was finished the next day, Charlotte took out her writing materials and sat down at her worktable. Sitting on the floor beside her, Margaret Mary was safely occupied with her doll and a basket of yarn. Charlotte was determined to write the dramatic story of Santa Chiara's historic chalice and how it had disappeared. She was confident that her American audience would find the story as fascinating as she did. The ending had not come yet, but surely that was only a matter of a time. Although Timothy and Marcus had not found the chalice, they had certainly discovered evidence of strange and suspicious activity by Lorenzo Tanassi and possibly his sister

As the morning wore on, Charlotte's thoughts kept turning to the abbess. How would she react to Isabella's tale of the mysterious drawings Marcus and Timothy had discovered? Would she go to the bishop

127

immediately? Surely he would want to find out whether someone was making unauthorized copies of the convent's treasured drawings. Were they being sold as originals? Or could it be possible that someone replaced the originals with copies and was planning to sell the valuable art?

It wasn't clear to Charlotte whether the bishop wanted to preserve the convent and its treasures, or whether it was more important to him to find an excuse to invite the monks to take over. What would it mean to him to have some of the art work returned? And surely if Lorenzo Tanassi was responsible for these activities, he was likely to be responsible for the loss of the chalice too. Or at least to know who might have taken it.

Isabella's talk about how old memories lingered on in Italy made everything uncertain. Would the bishop insist that the convent should be given to the monks even after the stolen chalice and other art works were returned? Were the thefts only an excuse for evicting the nuns? Perhaps the bishop was settling an old score against the convent. Trying to find the truth through the labyrinth of old struggles was impossible.

In the early afternoon, Marcus arrived with a note from Isabella. *"The bishop was shocked to hear about the drawings seen in Signora Rossi's home. An emissary will be sent to Pisa tomorrow to ask Signor Tanassi to come to Florence and bring with him any drawings or other objects that were taken from Santa*

Chiara. I will let you know as soon as I hear more news."

The next two days passed very slowly. On the third day, Isabella called on Charlotte. Her face was tense and as soon as they were seated she began her story. "Yesterday the bishop invited our abbess to meet with him and hear what Signor Tanassi had to say. She asked me to accompany her, because I am a representative of the Onofrio family."

Isabella paused to sip her coffee before she continued. "Signor Tanassi is a persuasive man. I had expected him to be contrite and to beg forgiveness for what he had done, but his demeanor was quite calm. He denied that he had taken any works of art from Santa Chiara. Indeed, the pictures in his storeroom were only copies of various paintings and drawings in Florentine churches. The drawings of the Stations of the Cross that Timothy told us he had found were nowhere to be seen. Signor Tanassi said he and others made copies of many pictures in order to preserve historic art that might otherwise be lost."

"Do you think Timothy might have been mistaken about the pictures?" Charlotte asked.

"It is possible," Isabella answered slowly. "But he seemed very sure and he has a remarkably good eye for art. And somehow I do not think either the bishop or Signor Tanassi are going to ask for Timothy's help in discovering the truth about exactly what he saw. The story about the copied art was just what the bishop wanted to hear. He nodded his head when Signor Tanassi said the convent was not strongly protected. And then Signor Tanassi went on to say that he was devoted to the treasures of Florence and wanted them preserved in a safer place."

"What did the abbess have to say?"

"It took her a minute to reply to the bishop's comments. Her cheeks were red. I could tell she was angry, but how could she show anger in front of the bishop? She argued that that convent was indeed a safe place. The nuns have been protecting the convent for more than a hundred years, she reminded him. I could see she was trembling with anger, but she spoke quietly enough."

Isabella paused for moment and Charlotte broke in. "Does Signor Tanassi know of the bishop's plan to take the convent away from the nuns? Does his family have a connection to the convent too? Does everyone in Florence have an interest in Santa Chiara?"

At last Isabella smiled. "It is difficult for an American to understand how much interest there is. And no, I do not know whether the Tanassi family has any connection to the convent, but it is quite likely that they do. During the days when my nephew was at Signor Tanassi's house, I talked several times with him and with his sister, but neither of them mentioned any family connection with Santa Chiara, although they did ask questions about the convent."

"Did the bishop accept Signor Tanassi's story without any questions? Did he ask anything about whether the copies were made with permission from the owners? Surely the bishop must have been angry to know nothing about this scheme. Did he rebuke Signore Tanassi at all?" Charlotte asked eagerly. "Did he mention the disappearance of the chalice?"

"There was no mention of the loss of the chalice. And there was no rebuke. Signor Tanassi has a golden tongue and he has persuaded the bishop that his motives are good. Perhaps he has even convinced the abbess that there are hidden treasures at Santa Chiara. He suggested to the bishop that he could spend some time at the convent, making more copies of the art works and perhaps portraits. Spending time there would enable him to observe and perhaps to discover how safely the art works are being kept."

Charlotte had to smile when Isabella mentioned portraits. "Perhaps he will at last have the chance to paint your portrait, as he has so often suggested."

Isabella smiled in return, but answered tartly, "I will certainly give him permission to paint my portrait. Then I will have a chance to question him about what he really hopes to gain from spending time at the convent. I am not sure why the bishop decided as he did. I do not think he wants many people to know about the valuable works of art stored in the convent. With revolutionary fever running high, the less said about treasures in convents, the better it is for all officials of the Church."

"Were these drawings the treasures your husband told you were hidden in the convent? Were they what he was searching for?"

"No," Isabella replied slowly. "The drawings of Antonino Pellarosa were not secrets. My husband believed there were other hidden treasures. I wish he had told me more about what he was looking for."

During the next few days, Charlotte pondered the strange turn the case had taken. Timothy was bitterly disappointed at not being able to tell his fellow art students about his great adventure in Pisa. He enjoyed hinting to them that he had important secrets he would share someday, but in the meantime he concentrated on his studies.

Several days of rain made the air chilly and deepened Daniel's cough. Charlotte stayed indoors to nurse him and make sure he rested rather than trying to work. He was glad to hear about the trip to Pisa but was just as puzzled as Charlotte by the discovery of the drawings and the arrangement the bishop had made with Lorenzo Tanassi.

On the first sunny day of the following week, Charlotte left Daniel resting on the balcony wrapped in a warm blanket while she went to Santa Chiara to visit Isabella. As she walked into the cloister, she saw Isabella sitting on one of the benches. Lorenzo Tanassi had set up his easel on the grass and was sketching the outlines of Isabella's portrait on the canvas.

"Do you mind if I watch you work?" Charlotte asked the painter, who smiled politely and murmured an agreement.

Now that Charlotte was faced with Lorenzo Tanassi, her mind was full of questions but she scarcely knew how to ask them. She wanted to ask about the chalice, but how could she question a man about a theft when there was no evidence that he had any connection with it? Instead she turned to Isabella. "Has there been any news of the chalice? Has it been returned to its cabinet in the convent?"

"No," Isabella answered, although she did not turn her head toward Charlotte. "The bishop has told us that he will continue the search for the chalice. He does not want anyone to hear of the loss and tells us to leave everything in his hands."

Lorenzo frowned as he listened. "The bishop is a very cautious man, but he has many friends both in the churches and in the government. I am sure you can trust him to find the sacred vessel."

Isabella raised her eyebrows slightly, but merely said, "We seem to have no choice in the matter. I cannot help but wonder what Santa Chiara would say if she knew of its loss."

"Please do not speak, Signora Onofrio," Lorenzo spoke quietly but his eyebrows were furrowed in a deep frown. "I want to capture the serenity of your lovely face without any movement."

Charlotte soon walked away from that corner of the cloister. She suspected Lorenzo was trying to flirt with Isabella and charm her into…into what? Did he hope to make Isabella forgive him for making copies of the convent's art works? Apparently he had already persuaded the bishop that he had done nothing seriously wrong. But what did he know about the chalice? His talk about protecting Florentine art sounded noble, but Charlotte had a niggling fear that he was hiding secrets. He had never seemed to be a religious man. Pietro Onofrio and most of the other revolutionary leaders thought the Catholic Church was their enemy. Why was Lorenzo different? Or was he? Perhaps he was not supporting the bishop.

Could it be that he wanted to persuade Isabella to marry him? But she was not a wealthy woman, and although she was still attractive and charming, that scarcely seemed to be an incentive for a practical man like Lorenzo Tanassi. Marriage among families such as his usually had far more to do with money and politics than with love.

Whatever his motives, Charlotte did not trust him. She worried that her new friend, Isabella, having been isolated from her family and old friends for so many years might not be able to judge the danger of what she was doing.

When Charlotte returned to her lodging later that day, she found a letter from Rome. After the long, discouraging visit with Isabella, it was a relief to find a cheerful letter from her old friend Abigail.

Dear Charlotte,

This will be a short letter. My husband has just found a carrier to take some of his papers to Florence and there will be room for a letter to you but I must hurry. I have been continuing my explorations in Rome and discovering many glorious works of art. While I have been studying and enjoying the art of the city, my husband has been meeting scholars and learning about the culture of Italy. It seems the French have recently returned all the letters and papers of the famous astronomer Galileo to Italy. There is to be a new museum built to house them either in Rome or in Florence where he worked. My husband is hoping to commission an English translation of some of the letters and publish them in America. He believes it will be the centerpiece of his publishing company and will be greatly appreciated by scientists and scholars at Harvard.

I must close this letter now. We expect to return to Florence soon, although I cannot tell you the exact day yet. We look forward to seeing Timothy as well as our friends in the city. I hope all has been well with you and your family.

With best wishes,
Abigail Baxter

CHAPTER FOURTEEN

Long, Dark Nights

It is a beauteous evening, calm and free,
The holy time is quiet as a Nun.
William Wordsworth

Over the next few days, Isabella's portrait slowly grew on the canvas. Lorenzo painted leisurely, or so it seemed to Isabella. Only once before had anyone made a portrait of her. That was back home in Massachusetts when she was a girl. She remembered the artist had sketched quickly, making very few changes even when his pencil slipped and her nose grew surprisingly long. There were many other young ladies in Boston awaiting his pencil and crayon portraits. But Lorenzo worked slowly and carefully and rubbed out frequently. He spent long minutes examining her face intently. Was he trying to make the process of painting move as slowly as possible?

Charlotte visited the convent almost every afternoon to watch the painting grow. One afternoon as she and Isabella strolled around the walls of the cloister while Lorenzo was busy mixing paints, Charlotte mentioned how long the painting was taking.

"Perhaps Signor Tanassi is enjoying the process of painting more than the accomplishment of having a portrait," she said to Isabella. "Do you suppose he is trying to spend as much time at Santa Chiara as he can?"

"Perhaps he is," Isabella agreed. "I have wondered myself whether he is attracted to me or perhaps to the treasures of Santa Chiara. The bishop is persuaded that he is to be trusted, but I am not so sure."

"Does he spend all of his time here in the cloister, or does he visit other parts of the building?"

Isabella thought for a moment. "He always works on his portrait out here, but when I go in to refectory for meals, he sometimes wanders into the chapel or the library. He has become quite friendly with our gatekeeper, Donato."

"He told the bishop that he would observe what was going on at the convent to see whether there was any suspicious activity," said Charlotte, "But perhaps we should keep a close eye on him. I do not quite trust Signor Tanassi."

Isabella sighed. "I do not know what to make of him. He is obviously a good painter and quite a charming man. He tells me that he knew my husband during the early revolutionary years, but I do not remember that I ever heard his name."

As Lorenzo set his paints down and started walking toward the two women, Charlotte spoke urgently to Isabella. "We must keep an eye on him and discover the true reasons for his interest in the convent."

During the next few days Isabella made an effort to be aware of what Lorenzo Tanassi was doing during the day. She strolled into the garden when morning prayers were over, brushing dew from the peonies as the sunlight began slanting over the convent walls. She heard Lorenzo's knock on the wooden gates of the convent and watched as Donato swung them open to admit him. Despite the early hour, Lorenzo always looked wide awake and eager to start work on her portrait, although that was not scheduled to begin until after morning mass had ended.

One morning, when Charlotte arrived with Margaret Mary to watch the progress of the portrait, Marcus came with her. He greeted Signor Tanassi politely, but distantly. He had already told his aunt that he found the bishop's response to the discovery of the drawings in Pisa unacceptable. "Signor Tanassi was very kind to me when I was injured. I believe he is a good man at heart. But what kind of a country is this where the disappearance of pictures and vessels from a convent is not investigated closely? Shouldn't there be some civil justice exercised? I cannot understand these people!"

"Italy is a far different country than the United States," Isabella tried to explain. "Justice is handed down from the Grand Duke or from the princes of the Church. All decisions are based on tradition and on the power of the ruling families."

Marcus was still struggling to accept the quirks of Italian justice, but as he watched the portrait come to life under Lorenzo's hands, he forgot his worries about whether or not the artist should have been punished.

"You have remarkable skill in portrait painting, Signor Tanassi," he said "When I saw the finished portraits in your studio, I did not realize how well they bring their subjects to life. You have caught my aunt's face remarkably well. Perhaps our friend Timothy should study with you if he wants to become an artist."

Lorenzo smiled and waved off the praise. "I have had a long time to practice my art. Young Timothy still has many years of study ahead of him. He too will be able to paint portraits like this one day."

"Have you discovered any new facts about Santa Chiara since you have been working here?" Marcus continued.

Lorenzo was silent for several moments as he carefully applied blue paint to bring out the sheen of Isabella's skirt. Finally he answered, "No, I have not seen anything unusual happening at the convent. Of course, that is not surprising. The treasures of Santa Chiara have been talked about for many years. Others have searched the convent before. Patience is required.

I do not expect I will be able to find anything of value quickly or easily. But there are mysteries here and I long to discover the secrets hidden within these walls."

That night Isabella did not sleep well. Gusts of wind made her shutters creak. The familiar sounds of the convent seemed louder and stranger than usual. Turning her head slowly from side to side, she stared into the shadows. Was someone moving around the convent? Her breath sounded loud in her ears and her heart was pushing painfully against her ribs, but she heard nothing else.

Remembering what Charlotte had said about the need to watch carefully for strangers—or perhaps for Lorenzo moving around—she slipped out of her narrow bed determined to see whether anyone was stirring in the convent. After lighting her bedside candle from the glowing coals of the fireplace, she slowly made her way downstairs to the door of the chapel. A skitter of noise startled her and she jumped when she saw the dark shape of a rat run across the floor and disappear behind the altar. Was that a bad omen? For a moment she hesitated. Prayers ran through her mind. 'Santa Chiara pray for me. Make me strong like you'.

She turned away from the chapel and toward the library. The door creaked as she pushed it open just wide enough to squeeze her slim body through. She seated herself at the long table, blew out her candle and placed the candlestick on the table. If someone was searching for treasure in the convent where would he go? The chalice had been taken from its hiding place. Someone knew where it was kept. Most of the gold candlesticks and vessels used for mass were stored in cabinets behind the altar of the chapel. There were also old and valuable books on the shelves in the library. Where would an intruder start?

Reluctantly Isabella tightened the shawl around her shoulders and settled on the least uncomfortable chair she could find. She would sit there until dawn awakened the nuns for their morning prayers. She started reciting to herself all the Bible verses she had learned as a child, and still her head drooped toward the table. No sound disturbed the eerie silence.

Dawn came and the clatter of footsteps in the kitchen startled Isabella awake. Next came the murmuring of the nuns making their way to the chapel to chant their morning prayers. As Isabella looked out onto the cloister, the rising sun had set dewdrops sparkling on the spider webs over the doorway. She made her way slowly upstairs to her room pondering whether nightly vigils would bring her any closer to discovering what was disturbing the peace of the convent.

The next night, and the night after that, Isabella returned to her vigil in the library. Twice she was startled by unexpected noises, a scuttling of small feet across the stone floor or a mysterious swishing that sounded like skirts sweeping across the floor. But no one appeared. She saw no light and heard no solid footsteps.

On the third night she thought she glimpsed a shadowy figure as she came to the bottom of the stairs. "Oh, who is it?" she heard herself say. Then her candle sputtered out and she felt something sharp against her side. She slumped sideways and fell to the stone floor.

When the sun rose in the morning, the first nun making her way to the chapel was Sister Lucia. She almost stumbled over Isabella's body. As the young nun knelt on the floor beside her, Isabella stirred and a low moan escaped her lips.

Sister Lucia ran to the kitchen where Sister Assunta was already bustling about heating water for the morning meal. Both women hurried to bring water to Isabella and to bathe her forehead. They smiled as her eyelids fluttered open and her breathing became more regular. As they helped her to sit up, Isabella gasped in pain and the nuns could see blood trickling down the robe at the side of her chest. Assunta and Lucia lifted her and helped her into a cot in the tiny infirmary next to the kitchen.

When Charlotte arrived at the convent later that morning, she was surprised to see no sign of Isabella or Lorenzo at their usual places on the grass of the cloister. She discovered Lorenzo as he was leaving the building. When she learned about Isabella's injury, she hurried to the infirmary.

Isabella looked pale and tired, but she smiled at Charlotte. "The nuns have been taking good care of me. A doctor visited me and dressed the wound with honey and herbs. Now I must rest while the healing starts."

"But how did this happen? Did someone deliberately injure you? Did you see anyone? Do you know who it was?"

"No. The stairs were dark. As I told you, I have been keeping a vigil during the predawn hours these last several nights. I have heard strange sounds sometimes, but have seen no one. This is an ancient building and there are unexpected creaks from old wood. For a moment I thought I heard footsteps, but I am not sure. Then came the pain and I must have fainted."

Charlotte's throat tightened. "Who would have attacked you? Surely no one is afraid of you. And who would be carrying a dagger in the convent?"

"The doctor said the wound is not deep. A dagger would have been sharp enough to cause more damage. This was just an ordinary knife such as any butcher or cook would have."

Charlotte stood at the foot of Isabella's cot. The room was small, just space enough for two narrow cots and a stand that held a pitcher of water and cloths for bandages. A knock at the door brought Sister Assunta, carrying a platter of grapes and cheese.

"Sister Assunta was one of the nuns who found me," Isabella said as she turned toward the lay sister. "You did not see anyone else near the stairs or the library, did you?"

"There was a shadow, perhaps," the elderly woman replied. "For a moment I thought I saw a shadowy figure run across the grass, but my eyes were fastened on you."

Isabella refused the food and she looked so tired that Charlotte soon left her to rest. She wanted to talk to Sister Lucia and see whether the younger woman had noticed anyone about the convent when Isabella was injured. That did not take long. Sister Lucia soon emerged from the chapel and was glad to sit on one of the cloister benches and talk to Charlotte.

"I did not see or hear anything unusual this morning," she told Charlotte. "I was the first one to go downstairs to help Sister Assunta prepare the morning meal. That is my task for this week. I often help in the kitchen."

"You saw no shadowy figure on the lawn or walkway?"

"No. The sun was not as bright as it is now, but I saw no one."

Charlotte thought for a moment. "You say you work in the kitchen. The doctor seemed to think Signora Onofrio might have been injured by an ordinary kitchen knife. Would you be able to discover whether any knife is missing from the kitchen?"

Sister Lucia quickly agreed. But as Charlotte walked home, she wondered whether she could possibly learn anything from a missing kitchen knife.

CHAPTER FIFTEEN

Discoveries

Then felt I like some watcher of the skies
When a new planet swims into his ken;
John Keats

Charlotte's walk to the convent the next day was purposeful. She had spent the evening puzzling over why Lorenzo, or anyone else, would attack Isabella

"Why would Signor Tanassi injure Isabella?" Daniel had asked during their long conversation. "It doesn't seem as though she would be a threat to him. For some reason Signor Tanassi seems to have the goodwill of the bishop. No one else would have suffered so little for having suspicious pictures hidden in his palazzo. What more could he want?"

"He wants to get into the convent to discover its secrets. There must be something there that he wants. Of course, from the way he looks at Isabella while he is painting her portrait I sometimes think he wants her as his wife. But that is hard to believe. She has been a widow for several years and gives no indication she wants to marry again."

Daniel lifted his eyebrows in surprise. "She has never been officially recognized as a widow, has she? Her husband has not been officially declared dead. Any change seems unlikely. Signora Onofrio is a charming woman, but I suspect our friend Tanassi would be more interested in wealth if he were thinking of marriage."

"Oh, Daniel, you have not seen his face when he looks at her. But I am afraid he may not be the kind of husband she deserves. He says he was a friend of Pietro Onofrio, but there is something about him I don't trust. Who else in the convent would have any idea of injuring Isabella?"

Daniel looked at his wife and smiled. "Well I don't know of anyone except you who could discover who the dangerous person is," he said. "But, Charlotte, be careful! If there is danger lurking in Santa Chiara, it might touch you, especially if you discover the culprit. And if anything should happen to you, I don't know how Margaret Mary and I could get along. You know you are the center of our world, don't you? You're what makes life worth living."

Their conversation had ended without either of them finding answers to the questions about Isabella, but Charlotte smiled as she thought of Daniel's face as he said that. She was still smiling when she arrived at

Santa Chiara. Sister Lucia was sweeping the floor outside the infirmary, but as soon as she saw Charlotte, she beckoned her aside.

"Something very strange is going on," the novice said. "When I went to the kitchen garden this morning to dig up potatoes for dinner, I noticed the soil at one corner had been very recently disturbed. When I dug down into it, you will never guess what I found—a perfectly good kitchen knife. It wasn't buried very deep, just shoved under the dirt as though someone was in a hurry."

"Did you ask Sister Assunta and the other kitchen workers whether it was a knife from the convent kitchen?" Charlotte was curious how the nuns would react.

"Yes, I asked and Sister Assunta said it was an old knife and had probably been lost for some time. She didn't seem very concerned about it and only said she would give thanks to St. Anthony for finding it."

The nuns may not have been worried, but Charlotte thought the lost knife might be important. When she considered where the knife had been found, the strangeness of it all struck her. How could anyone lose a kitchen knife in a garden? Knives are important and useful tools. No one would drop a knife and just leave it. No, this knife was buried. Someone tried to hide it on purpose.

"Show me exactly where you found the knife Sister," she said. "I wonder whether anything else has been hidden in the kitchen garden." Together Charlotte and Sister Lucia walked to the back of the convent and through the kitchen to the door that led to the alley and the kitchen garden. Unlike the well-tended cloister, the kitchen garden was quite untidy. The rows of vegetables were well-weeded, but around the edges, by the walls, plants were growing in profusion. Tangled vines climbing the brick walls hid the nests of birds and glistened with spider webs. This was a mysterious part of the convent that Charlotte had never seen before. She realized that the convent was a large complex of buildings—larger than she had known. And some parts of it were much older than others. The chapel and the library were not the only places that might have been used to store treasures of various sorts.

The two women walked slowly around the garden. "What is that cluster of stones along the back wall? The ones with some wilted flowers on them," asked Charlotte.

"That is where we throw the flowers that are pruned from the cloister garden," Lucia answered. "Sister Assunta likes to keep that spot looking beautiful. She said once while she was planting potatoes in the garden, she stood there a minute and heard an angel sing. She thinks there is an angel who likes that spot, so we put the flowers there."

When Charlotte went back to the infirmary to see Isabella, she told her about the mysterious discovery of the knife. "We will never know whether that was the knife used to stab you. And it doesn't help us find the person who did, but it has made me think about how complicated this convent is."

Isabella laughed when Charlotte told her that the stones in one corner of the kitchen garden were covered with flowers because a nun believed an angel sang there.

"That is just what some of the lay sisters might think," said Isabella. "Most of the nuns here are from prosperous families which pay a dowry when they enter the convent. But the lay sisters are often peasant girls who were taken in for charity because they were orphaned or neglected by their families. Many are illiterate and cannot read the liturgy or sing in the choir. They usually work in the kitchen or the garden and do much of the cleaning. They easily believe the stories that peasants tell about angels and devils and other superstitions."

"Whether they might be an angel's lair or not, there's something strange about those flower-strewn rocks," Charlotte insisted. "We should do some digging there to see whether anything has been buried. Do you think the abbess would give us permission?"

"You and I cannot dig there," Isabella smiled. "That would be a scandal. But perhaps we could get permission for Marcus to do some digging, or even Timothy."

That evening Isabella spoke to the abbess when she came to the infirmary for a visit. Ever since the injury,

Abbess Josepha had looked drawn and worried. She knew the bishop would use the assault as a reason for giving the convent to the monks. It would provide another excuse to push the nuns out into a rural area where they would be safe from the dangers of city life. When she heard Isabella's suggestion, her face relaxed.

"You do not expect to find more kitchen knives, do you?" she asked.

"No, of course not. But there are secrets. Someone is searching for something and I wish we could find out what it is."

Marcus and Timothy eagerly volunteered for the digging and started work the next morning. Two spades were found and many words of advice were given. Several of the younger nuns lingered nearby and cautioned the diggers not to accidently uproot any potatoes or carrots. Sister Assunta stood at the kitchen door, wiping her hands on her apron and frowning at the two young men. Her lips moved in a constant prayer and she shot many glances toward the sky as if begging her angel not to desert her favorite spot. When the hole began growing deeper, she flapped her apron at Marcus and angrily waved him away from the rows of potatoes. Finally she turned and retreated into the kitchen where Timothy could hear her muttering prayers or perhaps maledictions as she prepared dinner.

As the sun was setting, Timothy cried out sharply, "What is that? It looks like a shoe." He dug further and then pulled out a dirt-encrusted shoe. "How did this get here? It is a man's shoe. Why would it be here in the convent?"

Marcus leaned toward him and examined the shapeless, black leather shoe. "It seems to be a soldier's boot, but it is very dirty and moldy. It must have been buried for years."

Timothy hurried off to the infirmary to tell Charlotte and Isabella about their find, while Marcus continued digging. The dry, hard soil slowed Marcus's progress, but a few minutes later his shovel hit something solid. He leaned down and scraped away at the dirt. Was it the other shoe? But no, he saw the gleam of something white. And as he pushed the soil away, he recognized that it was bones—a human foot. He stopped working and stared at the chalky white bone smeared with dirt and with the root of one tenacious grape vine caught between the toes. What unlucky man had been buried here?

Charlotte returned with Timothy and saw how the work was progressing. Sister Lucia came out of the kitchen and looked down at the foot bones. "Oh, Holy Mother, what has happened here? I must run and tell Abbess Josepha."

When the abbess heard about the gruesome discovery, she sent for the doorman, Donato, and asked him to help with the digging. The nuns continued their quiet routine of prayers and singing, but a small circle of observers, including Sister Lucia and Sister Assunta, walked past the digging site as often as they could.

Finally it was clear what lay buried beside the wall. The skeleton of a man, twisted into an uncomfortable-looking position, was revealed. On one bony finger, Charlotte could see the glitter of a ring. She knelt down on the soggy earth and examined it carefully. Carved into the green stone, she saw a familiar shape, the Onofrio seal. Why would a member of that family have been buried here?

Donato crossed himself when he saw the skeleton and knelt down to say a prayer. With the help of Marcus and Timothy, he removed the bones and laid them carefully on a wooden trestle. Bits of half-rotted cloth clung to some of the bones, a sturdy leather belt sagged off the backbone. Everyone stood silently staring at the sight as Sister Lucia ran to find the abbess and report what had happened.

"We must call a priest," the Abbess Josepha decreed. "And we must discover who this poor creature might be."

Charlotte slowly stepped toward the abbess and said softly, "I believe the ring which is on that finger has the Onofrio seal on it. Perhaps Signora Onofrio will be able to tell us something about who this person might have been."

The abbess nodded in agreement and watched as Charlotte pulled the ring from the wasted bones and wiped away the dirt encrusting it. Together she and the abbess went to the infirmary where Isabella was sitting in a chair near the window. Her face was very white and it became whiter still when she saw the ring.

"I know that ring," she said. "My dear husband wore it always. Oh, my poor, poor Pietro! How could he have come to an end like this?"

CHAPTER SIXTEEN

Probing the Past

Time present and time past
Are both perhaps present in time future
And time future contained in time past.
    T.S. Eliot

When Isabella had recovered herself, she walked with Charlotte to the kitchen garden. Her steps were slow and faltering, but her wound had not become infected and the pain had subsided. When she saw the bones, still lying half-buried in the garden, tears gathered in her eyes and rolled down her cheeks, but she made no sound. Finally she drew herself up and said, "My husband deserves a respectful funeral. We must prepare that."

Abbess Josepha made hasty arrangements to have a coffin built. The body would be moved to the small crypt under the chapel and could remain there until a permanent burial spot was found. Isabella insisted that she no longer needed to stay in the infirmary. She

157

moved back into her room where she would have privacy to mourn and consider what the future might bring.

While Isabella mourned, Charlotte was thinking furiously about how Pietro's body could have been buried at Santa Chiara. It had been several years since he had disappeared. And at that time he had been a revolutionary trying to win freedom for Florence. How could he possibly have died in a convent—or at least been buried in a convent—even if his family had long been connected with Santa Chiara? No, it did not seem possible.

From what Isabella had told her, it was clear that Pietro Onofrio had been a loving husband. He would not have willingly left his wife and child. And the hasty burial in a kitchen garden seemed to indicate he did not die in an honorable way. Charlotte wondered whether they could decipher what had happened from the scraps of clothes that had been found with his body. Would those scraps offer clues about his death? Was it a coincidence that Pietro had died at Santa Chiara and that now Isabella lived in the convent? Charlotte would have to wait until Isabella chose to share whatever information she might have. Was it possible that Isabella knew more about Pietro's disappearance than she had told Charlotte?

The coffin was soon nailed together, and several nuns laid out the bones and the scraps of clothing that had been lying entangled with them as carefully as they could. Sister Assunta led the group that prepared the body. She carefully covered the skull with a soft black scarf and twisted a rosary around one bony hand. Pietro's coffin was placed on a long table in the crypt near the tombs of Onofrio ancestors. When Charlotte next visited the convent, Isabella took her there to show her the coffin, with a tall candle burning on either side. After the two women had paid their respects, they walked slowly back to Isabella's room to talk.

"All these years I have been dreaming of my husband and mourning him," Isabella said. "And secretly I hoped that somehow he might be alive. Now I have no hope left for that. My whole life will change. He spent his life fighting for Italian freedom. Somehow I think his death was part of that struggle, although I cannot guess why he was at Santa Chiara. I must find out. And I must avenge his death. But I don't know how."

"Your husband's body must have been buried years ago," Charlotte agreed. "It seems unlikely that justice can be done after so many years…"

"But I must do something. There must be some answer!"

"We'll try," promised Charlotte. "Daniel is feeling better today and wants to come here tomorrow to offer condolences. We will talk about what can be done."

The next morning when Charlotte and Daniel arrived, they found Lorenzo Tanassi in the cloister with Isabella. His face was grave and he was telling Isabella that the bishop was concerned lest word of the discovery of a body at the convent should be made public.

"He fears a scandal," explained Lorenzo. "He is not sure the body has been identified with certainty. The ring might have been stolen or lost. With so much revolutionary fervor in the air, he is afraid the exposure of a crime such as this will cause harm to the Church. When the Pope hears of it, as of course he will, he may be angry not only at the convent but at the entire diocese. He does not want to give anyone an opportunity to attack the Church or any of our nuns or monks. Whatever crime might have taken place, happened years ago and should be forgotten."

"My husband's death must not be forgotten," declared Isabella angrily. "Whoever did this unspeakable thing is probably still walking the streets of Florence. Perhaps there will be more crimes. We must discover who is to blame."

The two men looked at her gravely. Daniel was the first to speak.

"We will do all we can to help. We must write down the events as they happened and then see what they tell us. When was it that you last heard from your husband? Do you have any of the letters he sent you?"

Lorenzo soon excused himself. "I must travel to Rome to finish some business that is undone," he explained. "I will call on you, Signora Onofrio, as soon as I return."

"There is one more thing we should perhaps do before we look for letters," Charlotte reminded them gently after Lorenzo had left. "Isabella, would it be possible for us to open the coffin, so we can see more clearly what clothes your husband was wearing and whether they can tell us anything?"

In the chapel they found Sister Lucia kneeling not far from the door to the crypt. She smiled at them shyly while the rosary beads continued to slip through her hands. In the crypt, the simple oak coffin that had been made for Pietro was easy to open. Charlotte and Isabella stared at the carefully arranged body, but Daniel reached in and gently moved the discolored and moldy remains of a velvet cape that lay across the torso of the skeleton. As he lifted it, they could see a jagged cut from the shoulder almost to the waist.

"Whoever was wearing this cape, would have been cut badly," Daniel pointed out. "Look, there are some stains that could be from blood, although it's impossible to be sure."

"But the slash alone is enough to show that the death was a violent one," Charlotte added. "Pietro must have been hurt. He could have bled to death. But where did this happen? Right here in the convent?"

Isabella turned away. Charlotte and Daniel closed the lid of the coffin. They had discovered what was necessary to tell them that someone had deliberately attacked Pietro. Now the questions that remained were: Who had done it? And why?

"I cannot think about all this now," Isabella gestured to Charlotte and Daniel to follow her. "I have some papers to show you. My husband seldom had an opportunity to write to me, but I have a few letters and papers. One packet of papers in particular he asked me to save, but he did not tell me why they were important. Now that so many questions have arisen, I would like you to see them." She went to her room and soon brought back a small case filled with papers. "These are all I have. Perhaps you will go through them and see what you can make of them."

On the walk back to their lodging, Charlotte smiled at Daniel's renewed energy. His cough seemed much better today. Perhaps the bright Italian sun was curing him as the doctor had said it would. When they got back to their lodging, she urged him to lie down for a while and rest and he soon fell asleep.

Margaret Mary was playing with her doll in the kitchen while watching Maria shell peas, so Charlotte took advantage of the quiet to look at the papers Isabella had given her. They were in a small leather pouch, about the size of a book, which held four or five sheets of heavy paper with lines of handwritten black text. At first the page seemed a large block of writing with no breaks to indicate paragraphs or sentences, but gradually Charlotte realized it was a list.

On the feast of the Epiphany in the year of our Lord 1647, Bernadoto Gigliardo gave the gift of an olive grove next to the graveyard. Blessings be upon him.

On the third day after Ash Wednesday in the year of our Lord 1649, Eugenio Caruso gave the gift of 50 scudi. Blessings be upon him.

As Charlotte struggled to decipher the letters and numbers, she realized that what she held in her hands was a list of gifts presented to the convent two hundred years ago. Why would Pietro have such a list? He was a man of action, not a scholar. And yet, there was a familiarity about the dates. Where had she seen these before? Of course, on the notes that Isabella had found in the chapel. The list she had spent so much time studying, trying to figure out what significance they could have. Was it just a coincidence that some dates from this list of gifts were repeated on the mysterious notes Isabella had found? Where had Pietro found the list of gifts and why would he have wanted it?

Charlotte's eyes ached from staring so long at the black letters in the list. She decided to copy the entries that matched the dates on Isabella's list and see what they had in common. After copying three of the items, she realized they were all from the same person— Galileo Galilei. She recognized the name of the famous astronomer. But hadn't he been branded a heretic by the Catholic Church? Why would he have given gifts to a convent? And why were the dates of his gifts important?

CHAPTER SEVENTEEN

Danger in the Library

Truth is the property of no individual but is the treasure of all men.
Ralph Waldo Emerson

Sister Felicita sneezed as she opened another book. The pages were mottled with brown spots and smelled of damp and mouse droppings. Sister Dolorosa had told her to dust each book and to be sure to return it to its proper place on the shelf. It was tiresome work. The books were old and the dark black letters took odd shapes and sizes. Sister Felicita couldn't make head nor tail out of most of them even though she had always been a good reader. Sometimes she was even allowed to read the morning lesson to the other novices.

The next book she picked from the shelf looked even older than the first and the binding was scratched as though someone had run a nail across it, or a dull knife blade. She sneezed again and held the dust cloth against her nose to block another sneeze. The cover should be mended. Perhaps she should ask Sister Dolorosa for the basket of needles and tools for mending books. As she stepped toward the door, she almost bumped into Sister Assunta, who was entering the room carrying a covered cup.

"There's another pair of hands needed in the kitchen this morning," Sister Assunta said. "I've a bucketful of eels to be skinned. Here, drink this tea quickly and then come to help me. Sister Dolorosa told me the books can wait."

Sister Felicita took the cup gratefully and sipped the hot liquid. She finished dusting the book she was working on and returned it to the shelf. Then she walked outside into the sunshine with the cup in her hand and stood at the edge of the cloister sipping the tea.

When Charlotte entered the convent gates, she saw the young nun and walked toward her. "Sister Felicita, I wanted to ask you about something. Do you remember the day you fainted in the garden when you were leaving chapel? I hope you are feeling better now and have not been sick. Has that ever happened to you before?"

"Oh, I do seem to have some sickness on me once in a while," the young nun replied. "I think it is a punishment. Sometimes my mind wanders when

Abbess Josepha reads to us at dinner. God may be punishing me for that."

"When do these feelings of sickness come upon you?"

"When I'm busy with my work sometimes, especially when I work in the library. I am not feeling so well right now, although Sister Assunta just gave me this lovely tea. I was not attentive enough while I was dusting the books. I was feeling angry in my heart. Those old books make me sneeze. I know I shouldn't complain about dusting holy books," she paused to sigh. "But I had better get to the kitchen now to do my work."

Charlotte walked slowly toward Isabella's room. She had no news to give her, but perhaps together they could think of what to do next. The bishop seemed fond of Lorenzo and had apparently believed everything he said about the drawings in his sister's Pisa home. Neither the bishop nor any of his representatives had questioned Marcus and Timothy about the drawings they had seen. Was it only the fear of a scandal that kept the bishop from asking more questions?

Lorenzo had said he was shocked by the discovery of the skeleton in the kitchen garden, as they all were, but had he known anything about Pietro's disappearance? Could he have had anything to do with Pietro's death?

Charlotte was determined to find out more about what he might know. After she and Isabella talked for a few minutes, she raised the question that had been bothering her.

"When you first met Lorenzo Tansassi and his sister after Marcus's accident, you did not seem to know them, but now it appears that Signor Tanassi fought side by side with your husband during the revolutionary years. Did he know about your husband's disappearance? Isn't it odd that in all the years since then Signor Tanassi never spoke to you about it?"

Isabella's cheeks reddened a bit as she considered an answer. "I never met the men that my husband worked with. Many of them disapproved of me because I was not a Florentine and that was a barrier. My husband talked about only a few of his fellow revolutionaries. Signor Tanassi had left for England before my husband disappeared. It is likely he never heard about what happened. People were afraid to send letters about those events."

"You are sure Signor Tanassi was not in Florence at that time?"

"Oh, I do not know who was in Florence and who was not," Isabella's tone was anguished. "Everything was so confused. I was not in Florence, as you remember. I was still with my aunt in Assisi. Letters came from Pietro only occasionally. It was dangerous to move around Tuscany or to carry letters for anyone. Even now no one knows what happened. There are those who say my husband betrayed the cause and gave information to the Austrians."

Signor Bagnoli, Timothy's art teacher, had certainly said that. Charlotte remembered how shocked Marcus had been. Who could know during such a turbulent time who was supporting the revolution and who was not? It must have been like the years before the American revolution when neighbors quarreled with each other about whether to support the King or to form a new country. Many fled to Canada and some of the quarrels were still going on. But if Lorenzo had been in England when Pietro died, who else was there who might have killed him?

The bell rang for chapel and Isabella left to join the nuns in their prayers. Charlotte decided to go to the library and look at the books Sister Felicita had been cleaning before she was called away to help in the kitchen. It was easy to recognize the shelf she had been working on because her dust cloth was still lying on it, next to the books.

Charlotte lifted down the book next to the dust cloth and put is on the table to examine. *Sermons of Fra Girolamo Savonarola*, was the title. The name was familiar, but he had lived hundreds of years ago. How could there be any connection between his works and Pietro? Maybe she was wrong about the mysterious list of dates and gifts having anything at all to do with Pietro's disappearance. Were the gifts used to buy these valuable books? Was the secret treasure of Santa Chiara somehow linked to its library?

Charlotte's head ached with the effort of trying to connect the pieces. As she thought, her fingers idly played with the book. The binding was a thin leather that seemed almost untouched except for a roughness across the top of the cover. As Charlotte's fingers explored the surface, she realized that someone had cut the edge of the cover between the thin, flexible leather and the sturdy board that held the pages together. Why had that happened? It must have been done deliberately. No mouse nibbling on the cover would have made such a neat cut. Slowly Charlotte slid the tip of her finger between the board and the leather. A single sheet of paper had been inserted into the slit. As she pulled it out, Charlotte could see it was covered with drawings—incomprehensible drawings of circles with letters on them. What was she looking at?

After staring intently at the sheet of paper for a minute, Charlotte recognized what it was. It was a letter. The words at the top were a salutation to "Suor Maria…"

A shaft of sunlight as the door opened distracted Charlotte from the page. Sister Assunta stood at the doorway carrying another covered cup of tea. Did the nun have nothing better to do than carry tea to the library every day?

Instinctively Charlotte slipped the letter under the book from which she had taken it.

"Good day, Sister Assunta."

"Good morning, Signora. I have brought you tea. Reading is difficult work. Perhaps you should rest your eyes."

"I find reading a restful way to spend time. With this large library available, I am sure the nuns enjoy being able to read so many books. Do you ever read when you have finished your work in the kitchen?"

"My eyes are not made for reading," Sister Assunta answered sharply. "They cannot recognize those black scrawls. God did not mean for me to read, although He gave me the gift of seeing pictures."

"There are not very many pictures in this book," Charlotte opened it again on the table, moving it slightly so it covered the letter completely. "And thank you very much, Sister, but I do not want any tea right now. I must leave soon to go home for dinner with my family."

"Take it, take it," urged the nun, but she stopped talking when Isabella came back from the chapel and joined them. A few minutes later Sister Assunta left the room.

In great excitement, Charlotte showed Isabella the letter she had discovered hidden in the binding of the Savonarola book.

"That is a drawing of the solar system, isn't it?" Isabella asked. "A very old drawing."

"And it is a letter," Charlotte added. "Someone wrote a letter and drew this picture. But why was the letter hidden?"

As the two women talked they remembered lessons from long ago schoolrooms. The quarrels over whether the sun or the earth was the center of the universe. Isabella was reminded of one early morning when she was a child and told her brother that the sun was moving up the sky to peek into their kitchen. Her brother laughed and told her that the sun wasn't moving, but the earth was. She still remembered feeling disappointed when she learned the sun hadn't risen especially to see her.

"But why would anyone hide a letter about the sun or science?" Charlotte wondered. But even as she spoke she remembered that the Catholic church had forbidden people to believe that the sun did not move. The earth had to be the center of the universe because that was the way the Bible described it. Had the letter been hidden when such a drawing would have been forbidden?

The two women took down one book after another from the library shelves. The bindings of all the books were worn and it was not difficult to cut slits along the top. Although the bindings had been carefully made, the nuns who bound those early books had not had heavy tools. Probably the convent had not been able to send the books to a commercial book bindery, even if such things existed, so the nuns had done the work themselves. By carefully cutting the bindings, the two women found two other letters similar to the first one.

If these were letters concerning Galileo's work on the solar system, they would be valuable, Charlotte realized. Was this part of the treasure Pietro had written about? Were these the letters he was searching for? If so, he had paid a deadly price for them.

"I suppose we should show these letters to the abbess," Charlotte said to Isabella. But her voice was uncertain. "But what if the abbess thinks they oppose the Church's teaching? Would she destroy them?"

Isabella frowned and said nothing for several seconds. "Do they belong to the convent? They should belong to the person who received them. Who would that person be? It would be wrong to destroy these letters no matter what the abbess says. Now that we have found them after all the years they have been hidden, I want to protect them. They are historical documents. I am sure Pietro wanted to preserve them and would not have destroyed them."

"We are not living in the time of Savonarola," Charlotte agreed. "No one wants to burn documents now. The nineteenth century is a time of discovery, not a time to destroy the work of a famous scientist."

Isabella agreed, but she looked troubled. "We cannot put them back into the books. What shall we do with them?"

"They might be safer if we removed them from the convent," Charlotte suggested. "Perhaps I could take them home with me. No one would think of looking there. And Daniel might be able to tell us more about them."

The letters were soon rolled into a small package. As Charlotte carried it through the streets, she glanced from side to side tense with the worry of losing them. She was glad when the gateway to their lodgings came into sight.

CHAPTER EIGHTEEN

Torn Pages and Broken Books

Time will bring to light whatever is hidden.
      Horace

The rich aroma of pork and rosemary greeted Charlotte when she arrived home with her letters. Margaret Mary hurried over to wrap her arms around her mother's leg and Daniel rose from his chair to welcome her with a hug. As they ate dinner, Charlotte asked Margaret Mary about her dolly and Daniel about his book, but she said nothing about her own remarkable discovery until the baby was asleep and Maria had gone home to her family.

"Daniel, you won't believe what Isabella and I found at Santa Chiara today," she began. As she unwrapped the letters and spread them carefully on the table, Daniel caught his breath in surprise.

"What are these antique documents? They are not pages from a book, but the pictures look like some I have seen in astronomy books." He frowned. "Where did you find these? They don't look like religious documents. What connection do these have with the convent?"

Daniel listened carefully as Charlotte explained how she had found the letters hidden in the book bindings.

"The list of dates Isabella found coincided with the dates when Galileo gave gifts to the convent," she told him. "Two of Galileo's daughters were nuns in that convent. It must have been about two hundred years ago. Could these be letters he wrote to them? Do you suppose they have been hidden in the library all this time? And why would his daughters hide the letters?"

"Because Galileo was on trial," Daniel suggested. "Didn't the Roman Church condemn him for heresy? The letters were dangerous. Did he send them to his daughters in order to keep his ideas out of the hands of the papal court and the inquisition?"

"And his daughters hid them in the books they were binding for the library. I remember that Sister Dolorosa told us the nuns bound all of the early books. There were no bookbinders in Florence when those books were printed." Charlotte stared in awe at the letters.

"Is it possible that Isabella and I are the first people to discover them?" she asked. "Think of all the nuns over the years who have dusted these books and handled them and never knew they had a treasure in their hands. Do you remember what Isabella told us about how long people's memories are? She said that 'Deeds done three hundred years ago are still alive in people's minds.' Perhaps the daughters hid these letters hoping they would be found someday. If that is what they wanted, they chose a clever way to do it."

"They don't need to be hidden any more. The Church has stopped worrying about Galileo," Daniel said. "Even the pope has accepted the idea that the earth revolves around the sun. Didn't Abigail mention in her letter that a new museum honoring Galileo will be built here in Florence? These letters must be valuable now. They will be wanted for the museum."

"I must go to Santa Chiara in the morning and tell Isabella."

Long before Charlotte and her family were up in the morning, even before Santa Chiara's nuns had sung their morning prayers, Isabella was awake and dressed. She went quietly downstairs to the library and slipped through the heavy oak door. Early morning light crept through the high windows to brighten the room, but pools of darkness lingered around the walls. Isabella almost backed out the door when she saw that a small candle was lit in one of the darkest corners. A dark figure seated at the table bent over a large book.

"Oh," Isabella gasped when she recognized who it was. "Sister Assunta, I did not expect to find you here so early."

Sister Assunta blew out the candle quickly and moved to close the heavy book. "You thought I was always in the kitchen? God's work is everywhere in this convent, you know."

"Yes, yes, of course. I did not mean…I just had not seen you in the library before. And I hope I am not disturbing you."

The two women sat in uncomfortable silence for a few minutes. Isabella took down one of the books from the bookshelf and paged through it. She and Charlotte had been going methodically through the books, examining each one to find out whether the date on the title page matched any of the dates on their list. Isabella smiled to herself as she thought about a young nun, charged with making a binding for a new book, seizing the opportunity to hide a dangerous letter within the book's binding.

"Do any of the nuns still do bookbinding?" she asked Sister Assunta.

"No, no," the elderly lay sister replied. "All of the books that are given to us now are already bound. They are not new from the printer's shop. And if the bindings are damaged, the abbess sends them to the bookbinder. There are many workshops here in Florence now and the nuns no longer have to do that kind of work."

Both women turned again to their books. Isabella peered surreptitiously at the older woman several times and noted that she looked mainly at the pictures in the books. Sister Assunta ran her fingers across each picture as though absorbing the image through her fingertips rather than her eyes, but she paid no attention to the words on the page.

"Some of these pictures are lovely, aren't they?" remarked Isabella.

"Yes." Assunta spoke sharply. "The Godly ones fill us with good thoughts. And the Good Lord gave me eyes to read pictures. But some pictures are the Devil's work and I must watch out for those. The Devil can pull you down to hell if you look at evil pictures. That American woman. The one who is a friend of yours. She has been looking at the books in our library. She had better be careful or she may find more dangerous pictures than she expects."

Isabella was too surprised to answer. She wondered what kind of pictures Sister Assunta could have found in the convent library that would seem to her to be the work of the devil. And why did she think Charlotte might have found them? How many secrets could possibly be hidden?

As the sun rose higher in the sky, birds started singing in the cloister trees and the sound of the nuns' footsteps could be heard on the stairs. Isabella remained in the library, but she found it difficult to pay attention to the books she had chosen. Finally she gave up and went into the refectory to join the nuns for their morning meal.

Water was the only drink served in the morning, so Isabella was surprised when one of the kitchen maids came over and gave her a cup of hot tea. "Sister

Assunta thought you might want a hot drink after your work this morning," the young kitchen maid murmured. Isabella sipped it gratefully. Her concern about what Sister Assunta might have been looking for in the library faded away as she savored the warm drink and relaxed in the sunlight streaming through the high windows.

*****

Charlotte left her house early that morning, eager to see Isabella again and tell her about the ideas she and Daniel had discussed. Today was Maria's day to bake bread, so Charlotte took Margaret Mary with her to visit Isabella. The three of them sat on a stone bench in the cloister while Charlotte told Isabella that the letters seemed to be written by Galileo and sent to his daughters in the convent.

Isabella listened gravely for a while, but soon her head began to nod.

"Are you unwell?" Charlotte asked.

"It is nothing," Isabella answered softly, but as she turned her face, Charlotte was startled to notice that her eyes were unexpectedly luminous. Her pupils looked much larger and darker than Charlotte had ever seen them before.

"Are you sure?" she asked. "Have you eaten anything unusual today? Or had something to drink? Your eyes look strange. Like the eyes of someone who is using belladonna. But I know you are not a society woman dressed for a ball."

"I do feel a little odd," Isabella admitted. "As though everything is moving slowly and my mind is not as clear as it should be."

"The tea!" Charlotte remembered Sister Lucia's strange behavior a few days earlier and the tea Sister Assunta insisted on giving to her. Tea had been urged on Isabella too—on everyone—on everyone, that is, who was looking at the books in the library. Was that what Sister Assunta worried about? Did she know something about the secrets hidden in the books? And why would she care? She couldn't even read the books. She had said that God had only given her eyes for pictures.

Charlotte's thoughts were interrupted when Isabella said slowly, "Perhaps I should go to my room and lie down for a short time."

"No," Charlotte insisted. "What you need is some strong Italian coffee. We can go to the kitchen and ask for some."

The kitchen was warm with heat from the fireplace where a large kettle of soup was simmering. Two kitchen maids chopped carrots at the wooden table in the center of the room, while Sister Assunta slapped at a ball of dough, shaping it into a loaf of bread for the midday meal. Her hands were covered with flour, but she smiled brightly as she saw Margaret Mary coming into the room.

"Here, child, would you like a taste of my dough?" she asked, pulling off a small chunk to hand to Margaret Mary.

"We don't want to interrupt your work," Isabella said. "But if you have some coffee made, perhaps my guest and I could have some."

At a nod from Sister Assunta, one of the kitchen maids scurried away to find coffee. "Just wait in the cloister, you will soon have your coffee."

A few minutes later, Sister Assunta herself brought a tray with pastry as well as two large cups of coffee out to the cloister. She smiled at Margaret Mary and handed the two women the coffee.

"Will you sit with us for a few minutes?" Charlotte inquired. Isabella was still unusually quiet. The nun sat down and Margaret Mary came over to stand by her side. The child reached for the large beads of the rosary hanging from Sister Assunta's waist and Charlotte stretched her arm out to pull her hand away.

"No, let the child touch my rosary," the nun said as she leaned over the little girl. "There are blessings in those beads." The child fingered the round black beads for a few seconds as Sister Assunta leaned over her. Charlotte watched the nun looking yearningly at Margaret Mary and thought how sad it was that Assunta had spent all of her life in a convent without ever having children of her own to love.

As Margaret Mary moved to turn away from the nun, her eyes were caught by a ribbon around Sister

Assunta's neck. She reached for it and pulled out a long cord with a picture attached to it. "Oh, pretty picture!" she cried.

"Margaret Mary," Charlotte warned. "You must not pull at Sister's ribbons. Don't touch things that are not yours."

"She is only a child," Sister Assunta said. "Don't scold her. She meant no harm." But even as she spoke, the nun pulled the square cloth picture from the child's hand and began to tuck it back under her habit. Charlotte could see it was a scene from the crucifixion on a square of cloth.

Isabella had been sitting quietly watching, but suddenly she sat up straighter and her voice was harsh as she asked. "What do you have there? That scapular belonged to my husband. Where did you get it?"

CHAPTER NINETEEN

Confession Is Good for the Soul

The confession of evil works is the first beginning of good works.
St. Augustine

"Signora," cried Sister Assunta. "You must be mistaken. I am a daughter of God. I serve His holy wishes."

Isabella's face was strained and pale. She frowned and shook her head but said nothing more. Charlotte looked from one woman to the other, unable to make sense of what was happening.

"You are not well, Isabella," she said. "Drink the coffee and perhaps everything will become more clear. And, Margaret Mary, you had better play with your dolly. Leave Sister Assunta alone. Her things are not to play with."

Sister Assunta took the scapular from the child, cast a sorrowful look at the two women, and walked back to the kitchen, her head held high with righteous dignity. Charlotte took a deep breath and looked questioningly at Isabella.

"What is that picture Sister Assunta was wearing? I have never heard of a scapular."

"No, I expect not," Isabella agreed. "I had never heard of one until I came to Italy. They used to be worn by monks or nuns, but now they are also worn by other devout people who do good works. Many years ago an Onofrio ancestor was given the right to wear this green scapular for his work redeeming prisoners from the crusades. It may seem strange. My husband was not a religious man, but he was proud of the role his family had played in Florence. He believed his work in freeing Italy from foreign forces was a cause just as worthy as redeeming crusaders."

"There must be an explanation for Sister Assunta wearing this." Charlotte frowned in concentration. "Did she know your husband? Would she have met him when he visited the convent? Perhaps he gave the scapular to her."

"It is possible that they met. Sister Assunta has been at this convent ever since she was a young girl, I believe. But why would Pietro give her his prized scapular? He meant to preserve it for his son."

Birds were twittering in the trees and Margaret Mary was singing softly to herself while breaking a pastry into small pieces, but Charlotte felt an ominous silence as neither she nor Isabella spoke. Finally she drew in a breath and her voice was strained and hoarse as she whispered, "She could not have taken it from the body, could she? She could not have known."

Isabella frowned, clutching her hands together in her lap. "But she must have. She must know something about his death." She drew in a deep breath. "We must speak to the abbess."

At that moment they were interrupted by one of the kitchen maids. "Do you know where Sister Assunta has gone? The butcher's boy wants to know how many pullets we need this morning."

"I will find Sister Assunta and ask her to go to the kitchen," Isabella answered. She and Charlotte looked into the library, which was empty, and then in the chapel. Sister Assunta was sitting in a pew close to the statue of Santa Chiara. Tears rolled down her ruddy cheeks and fell unnoticed into her lap. Her nose was running, but she paid no attention and kept muttering in a muffled voice, "I have always served God. You know that, Santa Chiara. I had to destroy those blasphemous pictures. They are sinful! They would drag us to hell. I did it for you and for the Holy Mother."

Margaret Mary ran toward the nun and reached out to give her a piece of pastry. "No cry, no cry," she said as she patted the nun's skirt, but Sister Assunta paid no attention. Charlotte picked up the child and took her outside to the sunny cloister. Isabella went to the kitchen to tell the nuns that Sister Assunta was not feeling well and someone else would have to deal with the butcher. There were going to be far more important things to take care of today.

Charlotte soon left to take Margaret Mary home for her nap, but she promised to return in the afternoon. Isabella hugged her for a minute and the two women parted.

Late in the afternoon, Daniel walked with Charlotte back to Santa Chiara. They knew the news would be bad, but waiting was worse. Daniel was asked to sit in the formal reception room near the gate, but Charlotte was allowed inside and shown to Isabella's room where Isabella was pacing up and down restlessly.

"Oh, I am very glad you have come! Sister Assunta has been crying and praying in the chapel ever since you left. The entire convent is in an uproar. And the abbess would like to speak with me as soon as possible. Perhaps you can come with me."

The two women went to the abbess's large cell where she received visitors. Sister Assunta soon joined them, accompanied by Sister Lucia.

Abbess Josepha's voice was gentle as she questioned Sister Assunta. "You are not feeling well, Sister, but it is important for you to tell us about the scapular you were wearing about your neck this morning. I am your abbess and it is necessary for you to speak to me about it."

"It is God's work that I do," the nun replied. "He did not give me eyes to read with, but I can see pictures. I love to look at the pictures in the books in the library."

She looked fiercely at the abbess, her cheeks streaked and blotchy with tears. "My work is in the kitchen, but I can look at the pictures. And I can touch the books. I protect them. And that man was cutting our books!"

"What man was this?"

"The devil man with the black cloak. He came at night and he carried a knife. This was a long time ago. But he was cutting our books. And he had a picture. I saw it. He held it up for me to see. He was so pleased and smiling."

Her voice became hoarse and strained. "But it was evil. God did not make our earth a little ball. The devil man was so pleased, but I was angry. I picked up the knife and lifted it to make him stop. And then when I saw the blood I knew he was hurt. I dragged him into the little closet where the garden tools are kept. I thought he would get better. But later when I went back to get him, he had died. I did not mean for him to die. But he was an evil man and God must have wanted him dead."

Isabella's voice now came in an anguished moan. "And did you bury him? Did you leave him in the garden to rot in unconsecrated ground? How could you do such a thing? How could you?"

The elderly nun looked down at her lap and twisted her reddened hands. "I was afraid. I was afraid the abbess would make me leave and I would have no place to go. I have no home but Santa Chiara. I would die! So I thought I would let the devil man lie in the garden. I dragged him outside. He was heavy. And the sun was coming up. People would see what I was doing. Then the doorkeeper, the old one, Donato's father, saw me. I was afraid, but he helped me bury the man. He said it was the only thing we could do. He knew how hard life could be outside these walls. And I said a prayer for the stranger. Even if he was a devil man, he deserved a prayer."

A dead silence fell in the room. Charlotte felt a lump in her stomach as though she had swallowed a stone, and Isabella was sobbing quietly into her handkerchief. The abbess sat in rigid silence in her chair.

"Oh, Sister, you have sinned," the abbess said finally. "We must talk to the bishop and tell him what has happened. And you must confess your sins."

"Mother Abbess," Assunta begged. "Let me see my own confessor, Father Carlucci, before I see the bishop. Let me go to the chapel to pray before the statue of Santa Chiara. She will give me strength. She will speak to the Holy Mother for me. I was doing it for God."

By the time Charlotte went back to the parlor to find Daniel, her body felt so heavy she thought she might fall. "I can't talk. I can't talk until we get home," she whispered to him.

****

After Charlotte and Daniel left the convent, Isabella went back to her room to think about all that had happened. She remained in her room all through the evening meal, content to be solitary and think about what she had seen. But her thoughts were interrupted by the sound of footsteps down the passageway outside her door. Then she heard the chapel bells begin to ring and almost at the same time came a knock on her door.

"Sister Assunta has collapsed," the novice said. "The Mother Abbess would like you to come to the chapel."

Several of the nuns had gathered around the figure of Sister Assunta, who lay on the floor in front of the statue of Santa Chiara. But no matter how the nuns chafed her hands, no matter how many prayers they said, Sister Assunta did not come back to life. The doorkeeper was sent to fetch her confessor, Father Carlucci, and the nuns laid Assunta's body on a low table in front of the altar.

****

The next morning Isabella was glad to leave the grieving nuns to visit Charlotte and Daniel and tell them what had happened.

"Does Sister Assunta have relatives who will bury her in a family plot?" asked Charlotte. "Where does she come from?"

"She has no family. She was an orphan. The convent takes orphans sometimes, children who have been left on the streets. Most nuns, when they enter a convent, bring a dowry with them, but the orphans are accepted as charity. They receive very little education. That's why they work in the kitchen or as cleaners. But the diocese will bury Sister Assunta. There is a small graveyard for penniless nuns and monks and she will be buried there."

"Father Carlucci came last night to bless the body. And the doctor came," Isabella continued. "But nothing could be done. Sister Assunta died alone. All the nuns said a rosary and kept watch during the night. Tomorrow there will be a quiet funeral."

"Surely there will be an investigation," Charlotte urged. "There has been a crime committed."

"You do not understand how powerful Bishop Lucca is," Isabella explained. "The government seldom wants to become involved in crimes within the Church or its institutions. And especially in times like these I am not sure anyone will care to let the world know what has happened at Santa Chiara."

CHAPTER TWENTY

Death and Its Mysteries

For all that lives, is subject to that law:
All things decay in time, and to their end do draw.
Edmund Spenser

Father Carlucci said the funeral mass for Sister Assunta. All of the nuns attended and even the butcher boy hovered at the back of the chapel as the priest recited a prayer for the dead. "Have mercy on the soul of thy servant Assunta and release her from the bonds of sin."

Charlotte sat silently in the unfamiliar pew of the chapel unable to join in the priest's prayer for mercy. Why would the nun never be judged on this earth? Perhaps God could forgive all sins, but surely there should be some earthly justice for the murder of Pietro. When the mass ended, Charlotte and Isabella watched as Donato, the convent doorkeeper, and three strong laborers lifted the coffin and placed it in an unmarked ox cart for the journey to the cemetery. Then the two women walked slowly to a bench in the cloister and sat down.

"Sister Assunta will never have a headstone, will she?" Charlotte remarked. "She was left a foundling as a child and will be buried in an unmarked grave. What a sad life."

"Sad enough," Isabella's voice was sharp. "But she was evil—well, at least she did evil. She may have thought she was doing God's will, but my husband deserved to live. She had no right to take his life. I wish Bishop Lucca had not decided the crime would remain a secret. He has no right to do that. He is hoping it will all be forgotten, but I will never forget. I will keep my husband's name alive somehow."

"The bishop is more worried about bringing scandal to Santa Chiara," Charlotte agreed, "than he is about seeing justice done. He says we can never know for certain whether the body discovered at the convent is really that of Pietro Onofrio. Perhaps there will never be justice. Nothing can restore your husband's life. Sister Assunta is beyond punishment."

"He claims that the body has not been properly identified, but I know it is my husband. The bishop refuses to listen to me—a mere woman," Isabella's voice was bitter. "He says that many people wear scapulars and that an old and battered ring is no longer recognizable. Oh, sometimes I wish that I could leave this convent and all of Italy behind me."

"Why don't you?" Charlotte urged. "You could return to Boston with Abigail and her family. You do not need the Onofrio money. You could teach Italian and French. Bostonians would flock to a school where their daughters would learn to be elegant citizens of the world."

"That would feel like a betrayal of all that my husband fought for. Italy feels like my home now at least as much as America does. I no longer know which country I belong to."

While Charlotte was walking thoughtfully back to her lodgings after the funeral, she pondered whether she should mention Assunta and her crimes in the article she was writing. She could conceal the names and write a lurid story for her American audience about the murder of a young man by a deluded nun. Many people would be happy to read that. Most Americans believed convents were nefarious places and all nuns were deluded and probably evil. But knowing Assunta made everything different. She was a real person and Charlotte could not turn her into a vicious villain for an audience. Why did Assunta do the things she did? What if she had been able to read? Would that have made a difference? What if she had known the Pope did not agree with her that the pictures she feared so much were evil? But she did not know and so this terrible thing had happened.

"Signora Gallagher," a woman's voice called from a passing carriage. "May I give you a ride to your lodging?" It was Alma Rizzo. Charlotte accepted the offer.

"You look sad," Signora Rizzo said as Charlotte got into the carriage. "I hope there is no illness in your family."

Charlotte told her about the funeral, although she did not mention the discovery that had led to Sister Assunta's death. Alma Rizzo listened with sympathy, but did not ask any questions. She was intent on inviting Charlotte and Isabella to tea on the following Saturday.

A few days later, Charlotte and Isabella went to the Tanassi palazzo. Alma greeted them warmly. "Ah, we will have a nice quiet time to talk. My brother is eager to return to painting your portrait, Signora Onofrio. Several times while we were away he mentioned it. He had to visit his banker this morning, but he will be here very soon. He is looking forward to seeing both of you again."

When Lorenzo arrived, the Tanassis told their guests about the recent changes in Rome and what that would mean for the future of Florence and all of Tuscany.

"Now that the revolutionaries have given up all hope of victory, it is said that the pope will soon return to rule the city," Lorenzo told them. "People are going back to their old ways. Censorship has been restored and the aims of the revolution have been forgotten."

"You must be sorry to see such a thing happen," Charlotte said. "You and many other people have struggled for years to make Italy a more democratic country."

"Yes," Lorenzo agreed. "It is a disappointment. Many of us worked for democracy in Italy, but many others were opposed. Some people who said they were on our side proved to be traitors in the end. They wanted glory and wealth for themselves and their families. They did not want democracy."

"I am afraid that people here are not ready for democratic government," Alma Rizzo remarked. "My brothers, like so many others, must give up hopes of a new political system and return to the old ways. Ways that have brought prosperity and honor to Italy. Painting, art, music, all those will be supported by the pope and his government. The common people are not ready for democracy. We Italians do not have the same radical politics that you Americans have. But let us not talk about politics. We should appreciate the beauties of Florence and not worry about modern ideas of democracy."

"I must thank you for inviting me to Santa Chiara to celebrate the saint's feast day," Alma Rizzo continued. "And for me it brought a reunion with my friend who is now your Abbess Josepha. She told me all about the convent and showed me some of the wonderful works of art there."

Their talk was interrupted by the housekeeper coming into the room with a tray filled with wine and pastries.

"Good food and good friends are what make for a happy life," Lorenzo added, although when Charlotte looked at the lines of worry in his face, she wondered whether he really believed what he said.

"And you continue your portrait painting?" asked Isabella. "Both Americans and Italians appreciate beautiful pictures no matter what their politics may be."

"Yes, indeed I have returned to my painting. Perhaps you will come with me to my studio to see the portrait of you that I was working on before our trip. It has been quite some time since I have been able to work on it, but I am eager to take it up again. I hope to be able to complete it. Painting will perhaps make it possible for all of us to forget some of the sadness of recent events."

"Not all recent events have been sad," Charlotte reassured him. "Have you heard the good news about the discovery of hidden letters at Santa Chiara?"

"Hidden letters?" both Lorenzo and his sister leaned forward eagerly and Lorenzo continued. "Where were these hidden letters and why are they important?"

Isabella and Charlotte took turns telling the Tanassis about the discovery of Galileo's letters and how they had been hidden in the convent library. Lorenzo stood up as he listened and strode across to the window.

"How will the discovery of these letters affect the convent?" he asked. "How many people know about them?"

The intensity of his questions surprised Charlotte. Why would he care so much about Santa Chiara's letters? She quickly tried to change the conversation.

"I am afraid we do not know how many people have been told about them," she replied. "Bishop Lucca is sending a representative to the convent next week to examine them, but we know nothing more than that." She looked at Isabella after she had spoken, hoping nothing further would be said. She was still uneasy for the safety of those letters, which were now being kept in Abbess Josepha's private office at the convent.

"All of the information about the letters will be revealed sooner or later." Isabella smiled as she spoke. "But perhaps right now we could see your studio and some of your recent paintings. We will have to leave soon and I don't want to miss those."

Lorenzo's studio was bathed in clear, gray afternoon light that highlighted every detail of the pictures and sculptures scattered around the room. While Lorenzo showed Isabella her unfinished portrait and explained what he wanted to do, Charlotte walked around the room examining his other paintings. She noticed a number of drawings stacked on a table in the corner of the room.

"Do you mind if I look through these drawings?" she asked.

"Of course not. Look through them as much as you would like. Those are some of my trial efforts and all are unfinished. Please don't judge me by my explorations," Lorenzo replied.

The sketches were mostly of details of doorways or of furniture. Lorenzo must have spent a great deal of time in gracious palazzos far more elegant than his own. Charlotte looked carefully through the drawings, wondering whether she would find any copies of paintings from churches. These seemed very different from the drawings Marcus and Timothy had found in Pisa. Charlotte was struck by the beauty of a pair of candlesticks in one sketch, so she took it to the window to look more closely. There were jewels set into the base of each of the candlesticks and Charlotte admired the intricate detail of the sketch.

Her eye was drawn to a line that extended beyond the candlesticks, but seemed to have been rubbed out as though there had been another drawing behind them. Artists often reused sketching materials, she knew, but the extra line was a bit distracting. Something about it caught her eye—the shape of the curve—it was a cup of some sort. She tilted the heavy paper toward the light and realized that underneath the picture of the candlesticks, someone had been working on a sketch— one that looked very much like the chalice that had disappeared so ominously.

"Signora Gallagher, is something wrong?" Lorenzo was suddenly next to her.

"Oh no, I was just examining these lovely candlesticks. Even though there is no color in the jewels, I can imagine what a lovely painting they would make. Did you ever complete this work?"

"No, I had no painting planned for those. I made most of these sketches at a church in Rome. Someday I may use those candlesticks in a portrait of a priest or a nobleman. They would add an elegant touch to any portrait."

While Charlotte had been looking at the sketches, Isabella and Lorenzo had agreed he would visit Santa Chiara on Monday to continue painting her portrait. The two women left the Tanassis with many promises to see each other again soon.

The next day was Sunday and Charlotte and Daniel spent a quiet day at home with Margaret Mary. Daniel's cough seemed better and Charlotte was hopeful the Italian sunshine was working at last. She told him about the sketch she had found and her suspicions of Lorenzo.

"Why would he have been drawing a chalice and then erasing it? Did he want to be sure no one else would see it?"

"The thing that surprises me," said Daniel, "is that the drawings you saw today were all of objects, not copies of paintings. Did you ask him anything about the drawings Timothy and Marcus saw in the house in Pisa?"

"No, of course not," Charlotte said. "The bishop's envoy looked at those—or at least he said he did. I thought the subject too awkward to raise during an afternoon's tea."

"But it is odd, isn't it?" Daniel continued. "That the pictures in Pisa were so different. It is almost as though Lorenzo had two different studios to hold two different kinds of works. And one more thing, are you going to tell the abbess about the picture you found today? Would the bishop be interested in knowing about that?"

"There is no harm in drawing a picture of candlesticks or of a chalice. Those cannot be used as substitutes for the real items. No, I need to find out where the chalice is hidden and how it can be found," Charlotte insisted. "There are too many mysteries surrounding it. I must discover the truth and restore the chalice to the convent."

CHAPTER TWENTY-ONE

Voices from the Past

The essence of lying is in deception, not in words.
John Ruskin

Deciding to find the chalice and actually locating it were two very different things. As Charlotte went about her morning tasks the next day, she pondered how she could search Lorenzo's studio. Was there any time when she would know he was going to be out? What excuse could she use to get back to the studio? She imagined telling him, or his sister, that she had lost a glove there or a handkerchief. But no, they would hover over her like attentive magpies if she walked around the studio pretending to look for something. She would have to go when no one was home except perhaps for the slow-moving, elderly housekeeper. How could she manage that? And what if Lorenzo or his sister returned while she was poking about the studio. How terribly embarrassed she would be! More than embarrassed. She might be in danger. She was so used to thinking of Signor Tanassi as a friend that it was hard to imagine him as a criminal, but perhaps that is what he truly was—a thief and a dangerous criminal.

While Charlotte was absorbed in her thoughts, Maria brought her a letter. Charlotte seized it, delighted to have something to distract her from her worrying questions. She smiled when she recognized Abigail's distinctive handwriting.

Dear Friend Charlotte,

My husband tells me I have time to write another letter to you if I do it quickly. He has a packet of papers to send to Florence and the courier will be glad to carry a letter for me. Our days in Rome continue to be busy and happy. My husband is impressed by the work of many young Italian writers. He hopes to introduce some of their novels and poetry to Americans, as well as to make some of the classics of Italian writing more accessible in our country.

The Misses Oborne and I continue our explorations in art. Dom Giovanni is often helpful in showing us lovely works that many foreigners never see. Miss Violet Osborne was an accomplished artist herself as a young woman. I have seen some of the watercolor paintings that she did. Unfortunately her hands have now stiffened with age and she is unable to hold a brush or drawing pencil. She does not despair but has instead turned to collecting drawings and paintings. It is quite easy to find very fine drawings and small paintings here in Rome. I have accompanied Miss Osborne on some of her visits to these markets and have seen the purchases she has made. Her taste is excellent.

I have been puzzled by one painting Miss Osborne showed me recently. It is a picture of Christ carrying His cross on the road to Gethsemane. The figures are elongated and ascetic in a distinctive style. It reminded me very strongly of the Stations of the Cross you showed me in the chapel at Santa Chiara, yet Miss Osborne tells me it is an original work by an obscure Roman painter. Dom Giovanni has vouched for it and told her she is very lucky to have found it. I am not sure whether my eyes are playing tricks on me or whether my memory of the paintings I saw in Florence has faded. I wish Timothy were here to examine it with me. His eye for paintings is very good and his memory is sharp.

Oh, there are so many things I would like to tell you, but now my husband is urging me to hurry. The courier must start on his way soon. I look forward to seeing you before long. We will have much to talk about.

I close with best wishes for you and your husband and a special hug for little Margaret Mary. I hope she has not forgotten me. I look forward to seeing all of you again soon.

Your affectionate friend,
Abigail Baxter

It would be a relief to have Abigail and her husband back in Florence. Charlotte had become so entangled in the sorrows of Sister Assunta's death and the puzzles of the convent that everything looked gloomy to her. Abigail's enthusiasm about the beauty of the city would be refreshing. Perhaps she could even help Charlotte understand the disappearance of the chalice.

Less than a week later Abigail herself appeared, calm and smiling as always, and Charlotte was able to share the news of the past weeks. There had been no way for her to send letters to Abigail in Rome, so there was much news to cover. Charlotte quickly told her about Sister Assunta and her misguided attempts to keep the convent safe from the "heretical" pictures she feared.

"What a tragedy that she was unable to understand the value of those pictures. She knew nothing about Galileo or his discoveries."

"Yes, it is a tragedy," Charlotte agreed. "If only she had been able to confide in someone who could have explained to her that she need not fear the pictures. If only she had talked to Pietro Onofrio instead of attacking him! There was no reason for this terrible thing to happen."

"So many dreadful things have happened to Santa Chiara this year," she continued. "Their precious chalice disappeared. That was the beginning. It seemed a simple enough theft to start with, but the more I try to discover what happened, the more complications come along. The bishop seems to have decided that the nuns should no longer have the convent. He believes they are unable to keep its art works safe. I often wonder why he feels so strongly about that. This city seemed filled with beauty and joy when we arrived, but now I realize it is also filled with quarrels."

"And perhaps we don't understand any more than poor Sister Assunta did," Abigail added. "Timothy told me about the paintings, or copies of paintings, that he and Marcus discovered hidden in Signora Rizzo's house in Pisa. Where do they fit in?"

"According to Timothy," Charlotte explained, "they were copies of the drawings of the Stations of the Cross at Santa Chiara. And the drawing that your friend Miss Osborne found in Rome seems very similar to those. I don't see how there could be any connection, or how drawings seen in Pisa could appear in Rome, but it is all very strange."

"We must go to Santa Chiara soon," Charlotte urged. "You must look at the Stations of the Cross in their chapel and see whether the picture Miss Osborne showed you in Rome was indeed a copy."

A few days later, Abigail and Charlotte walked to Santa Chiara where they were joined by Isabella. After a few minutes of talk about the sights Abigail had seen in Rome, they entered the convent chapel. The women fell silent as they strolled around the walls of the chapel looking at the Stations of the Cross. Abigail examined each picture slowly and carefully, standing for several minutes before the picture of Christ on the road to Gethsemane. Then she turned to the others and gestured them to walk outside with her to the cloister lawn.

"I am sure it was a copy of that exact picture which I saw in Rome," Abigail burst out.

"Perhaps we should go to my parlor where we can have more privacy to talk," Isabella interrupted as they noticed two novices weeding in one of the flowerbeds.

Once settled in Isabella's Spartan room, Abigail continued. "I am sure the painting Miss Osborne showed me so proudly was indeed a copy of the one at Santa Chiara. What a dreadful shame it is that someone would misrepresent a work of art like that. Miss Osborne is not a wealthy woman, but I believe she paid quite a lot of money for a painting she thought was an original."

"And the question is who would have wanted to cheat someone that way? Who would have had access to Santa Chiara to copy the painting?"

"Many people visit Santa Chiara and some of them make sketches of the art pieces they see there. Our friend Horace Sumner has visited the convent several times since we introduced him to the building. He often makes sketches as do other people, both artists and students of art. I think Signor Bagnoli sometimes brings his students here to sketch," Charlotte replied.

"There is certainly nothing wrong with sketching paintings—or statues or any other form of art," Isabella remarked briskly. "The deception comes in claiming that what you have done is not a copy but the original. I am afraid that many people are cheated in that way both here and in Rome. And I am not sure anyone takes it seriously enough to punish the person who does it."

"Especially if they sell the copy to a naïve visitor from another country," Abigail added.

"The only truly serious crime that has occurred at the convent is the theft of the chalice," Charlotte pointed out. "I have a pretty good idea of where the chalice is, but we must find a way to prove it. And prove who is the thief."

"Don't forget about the death of my husband," Isabella's voice rose in anger. "Some dark deeds have occurred at Santa Chiara and we must find out who is responsible and who should be punished."

CHAPTER TWENTY-TWO

A Visit from the Bishop

Letters are among the most significant memorial a person can leave behind them.
  Johann Wolfgang von Goethe

The following morning when Charlotte and Abigail visited the convent, even the lowly daisies in the cloister glistened more sharply white and the fading roses had lost their drooping petals in the fresh breeze. The smell of baking bread and roasting lamb crept over the convent walls to brighten the hopes of beggars clustering around the gate. In the kitchen, lay sisters scurried from oven to table chopping onions and peeling carrots with red, work-roughened hands.

The blast of a horn announced the arrival of Bishop Lucca's carriage at the gate. The bishop emerged. His black cassock with its broad red sash and a long row of red buttons marching down the front was the visible sign of his importance. As he strode through the gate,

Abbess Josepha approached, bowed her head and addressed him.

"Your Excellency, welcome to Santa Chiara. We are honored by your presence."

The bishop raised his hand to bless her, and then beckoned the two monks who had accompanied him to come forward. Charlotte, who had been standing with her friends near the wall, gasped when the first monk stepped toward the abbess and bowed his head. It was Lorenzo Tanassi. But why was he wearing a cassock? No it could not be him. She felt Abigail stiffen beside her and heard the sharp intake of her breath. After the dignitaries had moved into the main parlor, the two women looked at each other inquiringly.

"But that is Dom Giovanni," Abigail blurted in surprise. "You remember. The monk who was so kind to us in Rome and showed me some of the greatest masterpieces in the city. He is a Dominican monk, I believe. I had no idea he had any connection with Florence."

"Not only with Florence, but with Lorenzo Tanassi. You have never met Signor Tanassi, have you? The similarity of the two men is breathtaking. Could they be brothers? They look almost like twins. But Signor Tanassi has said he is opposed to having Santa Chiara go to the Dominican monks. Why would he feel that way if his own brother was one of them? The longer I stay in Florence, the less I can understand it." Charlotte felt as though her head was spinning.

Soon after the Bishop and his attendants disappeared into the dining room with the abbess, Isabella joined Charlotte and Abigail in the cloister. She too looked as though she had seen something unexpected. Her cheeks were red with suppressed excitement, her lips were pressed tightly together and her voice was almost a whisper as she said, "Please come with me, both of you, I have something to show you."

She led them to her room, closed the door and pulled out a sheet of paper from the bottom of a linen chest. "Abbess Josepha gave me this letter last night. It was discovered hidden in the mattress in Sister Assunta's cell." She thrust the paper at them and Charlotte read aloud:

My dearest wife,

My thoughts are with you and with our young son as I lie in this dark chamber. Despite my best efforts our hopes for the revolution are not as successful as I wished. Our fighters need weapons to continue their struggle and I have been searching desperately for money to support our efforts. You will ask where I am, but I have been grievously wounded and my head is muddled with fever and confusion. The words escape my mind. It is a convent...it is familiar to me. I know this place. It has been a place of safety and protection for our women. More than a century ago one of them left important documents here. But they have been lost for many years. I have come here to search for them. I must find them. I must. But I fear my weakness will overcome me.

If anything happens to me, our son must carry on. Remember our dream of a united Italy. I have been called the Black Duke, and I see nothing but blackness before me. Forgive me, my beloved wife, I have failed the revolution and I have failed you...

The letter broke off abruptly without a signature, but Isabella's voice caught as she said "Now the bishop will have to believe that it is indeed my husband's remains that were found in the convent garden." Her voice became stronger. "I knew that it was Pietro. I knew it. Now he can be buried in an honored place in the tomb where his ancestors lie. Everyone in the city will have to acknowledge that he died a tragic and heroic death. He was fighting for Florence and for a united Italy. No one will dare say he was a traitor."

"Do you think Sister Assunta took this letter from your husband?" Charlotte asked.

"Yes, she must have. But she probably had no idea what it said. She was afraid to show it to anyone and so she hid it in a safe place."

The sound of the nuns chanting grace after their meal, "We give Thee thanks for all Thy gifts Almighty Father..." startled the two women. Hoping for an opportunity to speak to Bishop Lucca, Isabella led the way out to the cloister, only to find that the bishop and the abbess had made their way into the library already. Dom Giovanni was following them slowly, but then he suddenly turned toward the convent gates, which were opening.

Lorenzo Tanassi had just entered the cloister. He was walking toward the library when he stopped abruptly, staring at the monk. The two men walked toward each other and reached out for an awkward half-hug as they met. Lorenzo launched into speech, but the women could not hear what he was saying. Dom Giovanni nodded rather coldly and turned to follow the bishop into the library. Lorenzo walked toward the three women.

"So, you have met my brother," he said as he reached them.

Isabella was the first to recover he composure. "Ah, we did indeed notice a close resemblance between you and Dom Giovanni. Neither Mrs. Gallagher nor I had ever met him before, but Mrs. Baxter tells us she had met him in Rome."

She turned to introduce Abigail to Lorenzo and the two talked for a few minutes about the rescue of Marcus and the kindness he had been shown by Lorenzo Tanassi and his sister.

"My sister and I were happy to take care of the young man. We have both been looking forward to meeting you. But I am surprised that you already know my brother." Lorenzo looked keenly at Abigail as he spoke.

"We were fortunate to meet Dom Giovanni in Rome. He was kind enough to show me and some of my friends many of the most fascinating attractions of Rome, especially the art works in several of the abbeys and churches in the city. We had no idea, of course, that he was related to you."

Charlotte wondered about the coincidence of the meeting. Why had neither Lorenzo nor Alma ever mentioned their brother, especially because it seemed obvious that he and Lorenzo were twins? Florentine families always seemed to be very close to one another. Surely twins would keep in touch. Dom Giovanni must have heard the story of the rescue of the young American. Or could there have been a family quarrel? It would have to be a serious quarrel to separate a pair of twins.

At last Bishop Lucca, Abbess Josepha, and the others came out from the library . Everyone appeared to be cheerful and smiling. The abbess told Isabella she could have a few minutes to consult with the bishop and to show him the letter that had been found in Sister Assunta's cell.

The conference did not last long. Charlotte and Abigail paced up and down the cloister until the bishop swept out of the room and marched over to the convent gate, his entourage gathering behind him. Isabella soon followed, walking next to the abbess and both of them were smiling too. Charlotte realized the bishop must have agreed that the letter from Pietro was the final link proving that the body found in the kitchen garden was indeed his.

The two women finally had a chance to talk with Isabella who told them more of the good news. "Pietro's body will be formally identified, so he can be placed in the tomb where his parents and grandparents have been buried. It will be a great relief to have his good name firmly established. No one will ever be able to call him a traitor again."

CHAPTER TWENTY-THREE

Mysteries Remain

For there is nothing lost, [but] that may be found, if sought.
Edmund Spenser

On the day Pietro's body was buried in the family tomb at the cathedral, the large church was almost empty. Bishop Lucca did not attend the ceremony, but Father Carlucci gave the blessing. Isabella, all in black instead of in her usual blue gown, was the chief mourner. The nuns from Santa Chiara surrounded her. Charlotte and her family, and Abigail and hers, formed the small group of mourners who watched as the simple coffin was carried from the church into the crypt where it would lie beside other Onofrios who had been buried there for centuries.

Charlotte wondered whether Lorenzo might appear at the funeral, but there was no sign of him. At the end of the service, Charlotte noticed a silent figure standing at the side of the church and recognized Signor Bagnoli. Was he paying a final tribute to a man who had been falsely accused of being a traitor? Would all of Pietro Onofrio's revolutionary comrades eventually learn that he had never deserted their cause? Somehow she was sure the news would spread throughout the city. Men who had fought for the revolution for decades would take heart knowing that their leaders were faithful to the cause.

Perhaps she too could help to keep the revolutionary fervor alive. She could write about Pietro's struggle so Americans would understand that Italians were fighting the same kind of battle they had undergone themselves. Americans should not only appreciate Italian art and culture, but also understand how much the two countries shared in modern ideas and hopes.

After the funeral, the nuns returned to their convent, but Charlotte had invited Isabella and the Baxters to dinner. Isabella was clearly relieved to have her husband buried at last with his family as he would have wished. A feeling of solemn joy hung over the group.

As the meal drew toward its close, Robert Baxter turned the conversation to other places in Italy which he hoped to see. "Pisa's leaning tower, we have heard, is an unforgettable sight," he said to Daniel. "Have you and your wife visited that city?"

When he heard that the Gallaghers had not seen Pisa, he cordially invited them to go there with his family. Daniel protested that he could not leave his work, but urged Charlotte to travel with her friends.

"Margaret Mary and I will be well taken care of by Maria Spinelli. My cough is fast disappearing and you deserve a day or two of rest after all that has happened."

A few days later, Robert Baxter hired a carriage and a coachman, and the small group started on the road toward Pisa. Charlotte looked out of the carriage windows as she listened to the lulling sound of the horses' hooves on the dirt road. The Tuscan grapevines showed flashes of purple where the grapes were ripening under the warm sun. The rolling hills looked peaceful and they passed only a few groups of peasants walking from one vineyard to the next and one solitary shepherd, encouraging a dozen scrawny sheep along the side of the road.

When a group of ragged young men walked past the carriage, one of them with a wounded arm wrapped in a dirty cloth sling, and another hobbling along the road with only the help of a roughly carved wooden crutch, Charlotte remembered that the revolutionary battles of the past few years had affected many people. And those who had suffered the most had been the common soldiers from poor families in the region. The man with the wounded arm, his head wrapped in a red bandanna and his legs encased in homespun cloth, raised his one good arm in a prayerful gesture as he looked toward the group seated in the carriage. When Robert Baxter pulled the window open and tossed out a coin, both men scrambled in the dust of the road to pick it up and then turned and smiled broadly in gratitude.

As Pisa came into view, everyone leaned toward the window to stare at the church and towers in the distance. The famous leaning tower drew every eye and it was the first attraction they visited in the city. Then it was on to the church of San Francesco. After walking through the church, where Abigail sketched some of the statues, they went to a lodging house to have a meal and to rest.

Charlotte was determined to call on Alma Rizzo at her Pisa home. The chalice was still missing and Charlotte would not give up until it was found and returned safely to the nuns of Santa Chiara. Isabella might be satisfied to have Pietro's good name restored and his body laid to rest, but Charlotte was not. Abbess Josepha no longer spoke with great urgency about finding the chalice. Perhaps it was no longer as important to the convent as it had been in the past. After all, the Galileo letters, which they had discovered, seemed enough to secure the future of Santa Chiara. But it was not only the value of the chalice that Charlotte was concerned with. She wanted to discover the truth.

Timothy walked with Charlotte and Abigail to Alma Rizzo's palazzo. Charlotte was not sure Signora Rizzo was in Pisa and she wondered whether she would have a chance to examine the storeroom Timothy and

Marcus has told her about. As they approached the entrance gate, Timothy pointed to the church across the piazza where he had spent the night during his search for the chalice. He was rather proud of his adventure despite the failure of the search.

Alma Rizzo was at home and was glad to welcome the women and Timothy. "And is my friend Marcus not with you?" she asked.

"He is studying and writing," Abigail explained. "He hopes to complete a thesis for Harvard before he returns to Boston in the autumn."

Conversation continued over coffee and pastries, but Charlotte soon grew restless listening to inconsequential talk while her mind was full of questions. "Perhaps we could walk in the courtyard and look at some of the exquisite sculptures that decorate the walls," she suggested.

The sun was sinking and casting shadows on the cobblestone courtyard as the three women strolled around the walls. Charlotte looked at the wooden doors set into the walls and wondered which one led to the storeroom where Timothy and Marcus had seen the paintings. She did not have to wonder long, because Timothy cast a meaningful glance toward the last door on the right hand side of the courtyard. Charlotte moved toward that door, trying not to look too eager, while Abigail and Alma lingered over a charming Della Robbia roundel.

She had almost reached the door when it suddenly opened from the inside with a loud screeching of rusty hinges. The sound cut through the quiet afternoon and Abigail and Alma turned the noise, wondering what had happened. Charlotte walked closer to see whether there were more paintings inside. She caught a glimpse of heavy oak cabinets with several stacks of framed pictures on top of them, but her view was abruptly cut off when a man in a sweeping black robe came out of the storeroom.

"Oh, Dom Giovanni, how nice to meet you again," Charlotte greeted him. The monk was silent for a moment staring at her, but then bowed and smiled. He stepped out of the storeroom, shutting the door firmly behind him. As the door swung closed, Charlotte caught a glimpse of gold on one of the shelves. Could that be the Santa Chiara chalice?

There was no time to ask questions. Dom Giovanni and his sister were slowly, politely, but firmly walking with their guests toward the outer gates. There was nothing Charlotte, Abigail and Timothy could do but bid a polite farewell and take their carriage back to the inn where they would stay the night. As they jounced over the cobblestone streets, Charlotte's mind whirled with plans for how to find out what was hidden in that mysterious storeroom.

CHAPTER TWENTY-FOUR

Interlude in Florence

The life of the dead is placed in the memory of the living.
Cicero

While Charlotte and Abigail were on their way to Pisa, Isabella's quiet life at the convent was interrupted when Sister Lucia brought her an unexpected letter from Lorenzo Tanassi. He wrote begging her to allow him to call upon her. Isabella's first impulse was to refuse. She wanted time to recover from her grief and Lorenzo Tanassi was the last person she wanted to see. Quickly she dashed off a note politely but firmly telling him she was not having visitors for the time being.

But even as Isabella walked across the cloister to the gate to ask Donato to arrange for delivery, she had second thoughts. Lorenzo and his brother had done inexcusable things, but she was curious as to how they became involved. Lorenzo had been in England when Pietro disappeared. How much had he known about what was going on? Isabella hesitated and then turned

225

back to her room and thoughtfully tore up the note she had just written. Perhaps it would be a good idea to talk to Signor Tanassi.

The next afternoon, Lorenzo called on her. His face looked grave and for the first time Isabella noticed that his neat black beard was streaked with gray. After he had expressed his condolences for the death of her husband, their talk turned to the old days of the revolution.

"I was a great admirer of your husband, Signora Onofrio. I looked up to him as a leader. I believed in him. My brother, Giovanni, sneered at those who wanted to unite all of Italy as one country. He said many of the revolutionary leaders were more interested in their own family wealth than in the good of Italy."

"My husband was not like that," Isabella objected.

"Ah, I know that now, but in those days, all was confusion. I knew that your husband believed the revolution needed money to pay our soldiers and to buy arms. He had an idea there was treasure to be found at Santa Chiara, but he never explained. It was all a great mystery."

"Yes, I believe my husband knew there were valuable documents here at the convent. There was a family legend about that."

"I was not sure," Lorenzo continued. "And I chose to go to England with some others to see whether we could raise more money there. We seldom heard from our revolutionary brethren here. Letters were difficult to send and were often confiscated. I stayed in London for many months, but had only limited success. When I returned, our movement was in turmoil. The Austrians had gained a great victory and were taking control of the city. Many of our comrades had fled. Your husband among them."

"He never fled," Isabella cried out in anguish.

Lorenzo's face reflected her sorrow and his voice became even quieter as he continued. "I know that now. But those were difficult times and accusations were flying everywhere. My brother persuaded me that we had been betrayed. And he told me we should could find the treasure at Santa Chiara and use it to glorify our own family. That was how it all started."

"So it was you and your brother who made copies of the pictures and sold them to unsuspecting foreigners?"

"That plan was my brother's idea," Lorenzo explained. "He was sometimes sent to the convent with papers or messages from the bishop and he met several of the nuns. Our sister was a childhood friend of the Abbess Josepha. Gradually my brother was able to persuade the cook, who was naïve and ignorant, that he was protecting the convent from wicked pictures and books. She willingly allowed him in during the early morning hours while the rest of the convent was sleeping. He made sketches of some of the drawings and paintings and I was able to turn them into convincing copies."

"And why are you telling me all this now?" asked Isabella. "Do you think I can forgive your wicked suspicions and plans?"

"It is not forgiveness that I crave," Lorenzo began. "It is my honor that I want to save. I am not a dishonorable man."

The convent bells began to chime for vespers, interrupting their talk as the nuns began to emerge from the building and walk toward the chapel.

Isabella stood up and nodded at him gravely. "You have given me much to think about. Perhaps we will talk again." With that she turned and joined the line of nuns and walked into the chapel without a backward glance.

CHAPTER TWENTY-FIVE

A Tourist Seeking Treasure

The painter who draws merely by practice and by eye, without any reason, is like a mirror which copies everything placed in front of it without being conscious of their existence.
  Leonardo da Vinci

Robert Baxter sighed with satisfaction as he finished his coffee and smiled at Abigail. "Well, my dear, I guess it is time for me to meet your friend Dom Giovanni and see whether I can learn more about the mysterious doings with the drawings and the stolen chalice. Italy seems a far more complicated country than dear old Massachusetts."

"But you aren't sorry that we came here, are you? We have seen things that we could only dream about at home. You would not have wanted to miss seeing the Rome of the Coliseum, would you? Or the lustrous beauty of the Pieta in St. Peter's?"

"No, indeed, my dear, and I am grateful to your friend Miss Osborne and the mysterious monk she introduced to you. Now it is my turn to meet him. I hope he can lead me to even greater glories."

A few minutes later Charlotte and Timothy joined them and soon watched Robert climb into their carriage and start off in the direction of San Michele in Borgo. The street merchants were just setting up their stalls, and housewives were choosing vegetables and fruit from the food stalls as the carriage rolled over the worn cobblestones.

When they arrived at the plaza outside San Michele, the carriage slowed to a halt and Robert Baxter climbed down and entered the church. Only a few worshippers were gathered close to the altar to hear a priest drone through the prayers of the mass. Robert strolled slowly around the sides of the church, looking at each statue in its niche and examining the large pictures set high into the walls above them. He lingered so long studying each picture that some of the worshippers looked at him curiously as they left the church at the end of mass.

When he walked toward the main altar, Robert noted with satisfaction that a tall, slender man in a black cassock had noticed him and was watching him closely from the pew where he knelt. As Robert lingered by the altar, the monk slipped out of the pew and walked toward him.

"You seem a man who appreciates some of the art on display in our church. Perhaps I could show you more than what you see here."

Robert turned toward the monk and smiled, "Indeed I would enjoy seeing more. I have not been in Pisa long and have only skimmed the surface of the beauties here."

As the two men walked toward the West Transept of the church, the monk introduced himself as Dom Giovanni, a curator of some of the art works at St. Michele and other churches of the diocese. He pointed out some of the notable details of several statues and then led the way to the side door.

"If you wish," he suggested, "I could show you some of the other churches in this area. We are very proud of the artists of Pisa. Perhaps you have another day free this week. We could meet and take a more leisurely tour."

Robert turned toward the monk and then stopped and frowned unhappily. "Unfortunately I must leave Pisa later today. As much as I am enjoying Tuscany, my business calls me back to England and then to America. And I have not even completed a most important commission that I accepted from a friend just before I left Boston." He paused briefly and sighed. "My friend has been remarkably enriched by the recent discovery of gold in California and I promised him that I would purchase some Italian art for the new mansion he is building in Boston."

"Ah, so you are hoping not only to see our art in its native place but to spread its beauty to the new world?" The monk smiled encouragingly.

"That was my plan, but I have been so busy here that I am afraid my friend will not obtains the works he is so eager to possess. There seems no easy way of finding worthy art to purchase in Italy."

Dom Giovanni's smile grew even broader. "Perhaps I can help you. As it happens a relative of mine, my widowed sister, lives close-by. She has a number of beautiful drawings and some paintings that her late husband's family acquired over the years. Now she is interested in selling some of them. If you wish, I could show you some of those works."

"Could you do that this very day?" Robert asked as if unable to believe his luck.

"This very day. Just come with me."

The two men were soon at Alma Rizzo's palazzo where Dom Giovanni led the way to the storage room adjacent to the courtyard.

****

On the other side of the piazza, outside the looming church a sharp-eyed young boy watched as Dom Giovanni and his new friend entered the gate of the Rizzo palazzo. As soon as the gate closed behind them, the boy entered the church and walked over to two women who sat together at a pew near the back. A quick nod of the head and the two women rose to follow him out of the church and toward the palazzo.

Charlotte and Abigail were dressed for an afternoon call and the *patrone* who guarded the door remembered them from the day before and quickly admitted them. Timothy trailed behind. Instead of following the gatekeeper toward the staircase leading up to the living quarters, the small group turned toward the storage room. The door was still open to allow more light to fall upon the drawings that lined the shelves. The women saw two men standing beside a long wooden table. Robert Baxter was watching as the monk lit a candle to bring more light into the dim storage room.

"Good morning, Dom Giovanni," Charlotte said as she bent her head slightly to enter through the low door. Abigail walked quickly toward Robert and took her husband's arm. Robert smiled and greeted them. "I have met your friend Dom Giovanni," he told them unnecessarily.

Dom Giovanni paused only a second before speaking to Abigail. "Ah, Signora Baxter, I did not realize that I had met your husband. It is indeed an honor. I thought you and your family were in Florence."

"We are on a short trip to Pisa," Robert explained. "And I am most eager to see those pictures you were telling me about. Am I correct in thinking they are in this cabinet?" The last words were spoken as he started walking resolutely toward the large, dark wooden cabinet against the wall.

"Perhaps we can wait for another day," Dom Giovanni suggested quickly. "We do not want to tire the ladies."

"Oh no," Abigail insisted. "As my husband says, we are most anxious to see the pictures as soon as possible."

Dom Giovanni reluctantly reached toward one of the drawers and pulled it open. All they could see was a roughly textured linen cloth, but as the monk slowly turned back the cloth, several small paintings came into sight. The light was dim and it was difficult to see the pictures clearly, but as Dom Giovanni raised the candle higher, Timothy stepped toward the drawer and drew his breath in sharply. Now he recognized the pictures.

"These are some of the pictures I saw at Santa Chiara," he said. "Or they are excellent copies of them. I certainly remember that Madonna holding a daisy close to the baby's chin. I am sure these are the same."

"But I thought I had made clear that I wanted original pictures not copies." Robert Baxter frowned as he spoke. "Genuine heirlooms that were being sold by the owners. Did you not tell me that many families and monasteries are selling original art works they have held for centuries? Are these copies? Or," he added as though he had just thought of it, "perhaps they are stolen? Surely that cannot be true."

"Of course that is not true," Dom Giovanni was almost shouting now and his speech became more unintelligible as he switched to Italian and spoke so rapidly that none of the visitors could understand him.

The loud voice startled the cook in the kitchen across the courtyard and half a dozen servants appeared from various parts of the palazzo. Several started talking at once, but their voices lowered as they heard a clear voice from the upper rooms.

"What is going on?" demanded Alma Rizzo as she descended the stone staircase from the family quarters. "Why are you not carrying on your work?" she asked the servants as she walked toward her brother and the visitors standing outside the storeroom. "And how is it I was not informed that we had visitors?" She glared at the Baxters and Charlotte who had come out of the storeroom and were staring at the ongoing drama.

Dom Giovanni stood in the doorway of the storeroom as if he was guarding it, but he no longer held the candle. Timothy, who was more interested in the pictures than in arguments, saw a thin blue wisp of smoke curl out over the monk's head.

"He's burning them! He has started a fire!" Timothy called loudly as he moved toward the storeroom door. Robert Baxter followed him quickly and Charlotte was right behind. Dom Giovanni instinctively stepped back as they approached and the doorway was cleared.

"Fire! Fire!" shouted the cook as she and one of the kitchen maids began to vigorously pump water from the courtyard well and a stable hand carried a bucket toward the storeroom.

The fire was soon extinguished, but many of the drawings were so wet and damaged they would never be of any value again. Abigail leaned over the drawer and touched the edges of the sodden paper. Her eyes filled with tears at the loss.

"It is all right, Signora Baxter," Dom Giovanni said softly. "They are only copies. The originals are safe still at Santa Chiara. My brother and I were trying…" . He paused and began again, "We were only trying to bring back the glory of the Tanassi family and save the treasures that belong to Santa Chiara and to Florence. Perhaps we were wrong."

"Dom Giovanni, I trusted you," Abigail said sadly. "You know so much about art and beauty. How could you have practiced such deception?"

CHAPTER TWENTY-SIX

The Past Is With Us Always

Fear not for the future, weep not for the past.
Percy Bysshe Shelley

Charlotte fidgeted in her seat on the trip back to Florence, wondering why the horses moved so slowly. Now that the excitement was over, all she could think about was being with Margaret Mary and Daniel again. She had seen Pisa. More important, she had discovered the mysterious storeroom and the secrets it held. The mystery of what had happened to Santa Chiara's pictures was over. That was a relief. Surely Dom Giovanni would have to face the bishop and explain what he had done.

But that did not mean she was completely satisfied. The chalice was still missing. Despite her plans and hopes, she had not discovered it. She was sure Lorenzo had something to do with its disappearance, but how could she find the treasure and reveal the crime? None of her efforts so far had unearthed the chalice. Her work was not yet finished.

The sun was sinking behind them, casting the dark shadow of the carriage on the road before them as Charlotte and her friends neared Florence. One horse shied and tossed its head as a hare skittered across the road and disappeared into the grapevines. Timothy smiled to himself, remembering no doubt how clever he had been to identify the drawings. But Charlotte felt dissatisfied and restless, thinking of tasks still undone.

All traces of melancholy disappeared when the carriage arrived at the Gallagher's lodgings. Abigail kissed Charlotte and promised to call on her the next day. And Robert Baxter escorted her to the door where Daniel and Margaret Mary were waiting to greet her. The child's tiny fingers clung to her skirt while Daniel's arm encircled her shoulder. Charlotte finally forgot about the chalice as she told both of them about her adventures.

The following afternoon Abigail kept her promise to call on Charlotte. The two of them agreed to go to Santa Chiara and call on Isabella. As the three women settled into chairs in Isabella's parlor, Charlotte explained what they had discovered in Pisa.

Isabella was not as surprised as Charlotte had expected. "There have been some developments here while you were in Pisa," she told them. "I have learned much about Dom Giovanni. Lorenzo Tanassi visited me this week and told me about the scheme he and his brother had devised. Dom Giovanni came to the convent and copied the drawings and his brother perfected them for sale."

"But how did Dom Giovanni gain access to the convent?" asked Charlotte.

"It seems that Sister Assunta was in the habit of going to the kitchen immediately after the nuns finished their matins prayer. She would poke the kitchen fire to be sure it did not go out before dawn. Dom Giovanni in his long black cassock could easily persuade her that he was a godly figure sent to protect the convent from heretical works. Sister Assunta would let him into the library where he could work by the light of candles to copy the drawings.

"And poor Sister Assunta thought she was doing it for the greater glory of God and the convent." Isabella looked grave as she spoke. "The poor deluded woman had thought my husband was searching for evil, heretical documents, but Dom Giovanni somehow persuaded her that he was a force for good. If only she had tried to find wiser guidance from the abbess."

"I suspect," Charlotte added, "that Sister Assunta was still feeling terrible guilt about the death of your husband. She probably believed she was somehow making up for that by helping a man who was copying holy drawings."

"But what about the chalice?" Isabella suddenly asked. "Was there any sign of that in Dom Giovanni's storage room?"

"No sign at all that we saw. Of course we could not search the entire room. We are not police. All we can do is tell Abbess Josepha and Bishop Lucca what was going on with the drawings. We still have no proof there is any connection with the chalice." Charlotte replied.

"How large was that chalice?" Abigail asked. "Would it be difficult to hide? Where was it kept for all the years that the convent owned it? Was it always hidden away? Most of the chalices and other sacred vessels are kept in the chapel surely."

"The Santa Chiara chalice was considered especially valuable. That is why it was kept separately from the others. Come, I will show you. Its hiding place was a well-kept secret, but now that it has been lost, I suppose it doesn't matter who knows the spot." Isabella led the way and showed Abigail the drawing of an earth-centered universe still hanging on the wall in the library near one of the bookcases. "See, this picture swings back and reveals a small cubby hole that must have been made many years ago." She pushed the picture aside with her hand and brushed away the curtain over the hiding hole. Suddenly the three of them were speechless. The magnificent golden chalice with all its jewels gleamed before their eyes.

"Is someone playing tricks with us?" Charlotte bristled at the thought that they might be fooled just as Sister Assunta had been.

"We must take it to Abbess Josepha," Isabella said, reaching for the chalice. But then she changed her mind. "No, we had better not touch it. We will inform the abbess about what has happened and ask her to come and see it for herself."

Soon the small library was filled with nuns crowding around, standing on tip-toe, trying to see the chalice that had been miraculously returned.

"Oh, I think an angel must have come down to return our precious chalice to us," breathed Sister Lucia to several novices. "Our prayers have been answered. Surely this is a sign of God's blessing."

Abbess Josepha decided that special prayers of thanksgiving should be said, and as the nuns filed into the chapel, Isabella led her friends back to the quiet parlor where they had been visiting. Charlotte felt a sense of foreboding as she faced the other two.

"How did the chalice reappear here?" she asked frowning. "I had hoped to solve this mystery, but instead it just grows and grows. Sister Lucia talks of angels, but it was no angel who took the chalice and then brought it back."

"And I am sure it was no devil either," Isabella laughed quietly. "Someone human has had a change of heart. If Timothy caught a glimpse of the chalice in

Pisa, and you saw a drawing of it in Lorenzo's studio, who do you think that human could be?"

"You are right. We must speak to Lorenzo Tanassi. He must be the key to this," Charlotte agreed. "He is the one who seems to be at the center of this affair. We know that Dom Giovanni spent time in the library while he was copying the drawings. And his brother knew about that. He would have had a chance to take the chalice too. They worked together on the whole outrageous project. Do you think that both of them wanted to return it?"

"I know nothing about Dom Giovanni's heart," Isabella replied, "But you may read the note I received from Lorenzo Tanassi last evening. I was waiting to show it to you." She drew a piece of paper out of her pocket and handed it to Charlotte, who quickly read it aloud.

My dear Signora Onofrio,

I know that I can claim no favor from you. After all that you have learned, including many things of which I am ashamed, I can expect no pardon. Nonetheless, I shall beg you for the favor of letting me complete the portrait I started weeks ago.

For several years my heart has been bitter because of the betrayal of a man I trusted as a friend and supporter of our mutual dreams of a united Italy. In my bitterness I felt justified in placing my interests above those of our cause and trying to enrich myself at the expense of others. Now I have discovered there was no betrayal. The man I judged so harshly was guilty of no evil deed. As you know, that was your husband, Pietro Onofrio. My only hope is that I can make some amends for my suspicions. I know that it will take time for you to begin to trust me again, but perhaps if we can spend some time together I will have an opportunity to show you how much I regret many of my actions.

If you will do me the favor of allowing me to continue work, I will be ready to start on any day that you propose. I await your answer.

Your faithful servant,

Lorenzo Tanassi

The three women looked at each other in sudden understanding.

***

The weeks that followed the trip to Pisa rolled slowly by. Florence was moving into the languid heat of July. Birds chirped quietly in the afternoon heat and bees buzzed sleepily as they moved among the flowers in the cloister. Lorenzo Tanassi resumed his visits to the cloister and spent long hours working on his portrait of Isabella. After the sessions he and Isabella would take tea and once or twice the Abbess Josepha joined them. Even she began to forgive him for the wrongs he had done to the convent. As she admitted to Isabella, it was the deeds of the Tanassi brothers that gradually brought about the discovery of the Galileo letters. These were already causing a stir in the diocese

244 | ADELE FASICK

and as far away as Rome. Their importance reflected well on the convent.

Dom Giovanni did not fare so well. It was he who had devised the scheme for using the convent's drawings in a dishonest plan to cheat foreigners. He was the one who had tricked poor Sister Assunta into believing she was doing the right thing by serving belladonna tea to the young nuns to prevent the discovery of the heretical drawings she so feared. And Dom Giovanni had not done it to serve a higher cause like the revolution. His motive was greed. He wanted to turn back the years and have his family glorified and allow the Dominican brothers take over the convent. Before the summer was over he was quietly reassigned to a small monastery in the mountains where he would no longer have the opportunity to turn sacred art into profits for himself and his colleagues.

****

One day when summer was almost over, a messenger arrived at the convent with a letter from Bishop Lucca. He would visit Santa Chiara to officially accept the Galileo letters discovered at the convent. Abbess Josepha decided to celebrate with a reception to which she invited the Gallaghers and the Baxters as well as Marcus and Timothy. Everyone gathered in the cloister for the bishop's blessing. After he had left with his entourage, the nuns emerged from the chapel and mingled with their guests as they celebrated the new security they felt in their home.

Afterward as the Americans walked back to their lodgings, Charlotte and Daniel had their own good news to share with their friends. Daniel's doctor had told him that his consumption had been overcome. His cough had disappeared and his lungs seemed stronger. He and Charlotte could plan their future with confidence.

As for Charlotte, she had received a letter from Horace Greeley praising her article about Florence and Santa Chiara. He offered her a contract to provide other articles about Italy, as many as she could manage, and told her that he looked forward to a long series of publications.

Robert Baxter also had news. He told his friends that he would be taking his family back to Boston within a few weeks. "Europe has been a revelation to me," he declared. "The beauty of the art here is almost unbelievable and the history is overwhelming. Now it is time for us Americans to develop our own culture and record our own history. The past has much to show us, but we are halfway through the nineteenth century and we should look forward to building a new future on the other side of the ocean."

Charlotte felt Daniel's arm tighten around her shoulder. She knew he was thinking that they too could return to America and continue their life there. Both of them were young and strong and they too would be part of America's future.

Afterword

Characters Based on Real People

This book is a work of fiction, but several of the characters mentioned in it are based on real people who were living in Florence during the 1840s. Chief among them is MARGARET FULLER, who has made a cameo appearance in every one of the stories in the CHARLOTTE EDGERTON MYSTERY series. The location of each book in the series mirrors the places where Margaret Fuller spent time during the year covered in the book. *A Death in Utopia* is set in Brook Farm in Massachusetts, which Fuller frequently visited. The action of *Death Visits a Bawdy House* takes place during the years when Fuller lived in New York. *Death Calls at the Palace* coincides with the years when she was in Europe and spent some time in London. This volume, *Death Enters the Conve*nt, is set during Fuller's last years when she lived in Rome and then in Florence with her husband GIOVANNI OSSOLI and her infant child. In 1850, the year after the events in this book, Fuller, with her husband and child, set out on the long voyage back to America. HORACE SUMNER travelled with them. All four of them died when the ship that carried them sank off the shore of Long Island. Readers can find out more about Margaret Fuller in my 2012 biography of her *Margaret Fuller: An Uncommon Woman.*

Several of the characters introduced at the party in Chapter Eight were real people. These include the well-known sculptor HORATIO GREENOUGH and his wife, as well as HORACE SUMNER, brother of Senator Charles Sumner, a forceful voice for the anti-slavery forces in Congress. LEWIS CASS, JR. was well known among Americans living in Florence at this time. He served in the diplomatic corps in Rome and Florence during the Italian revolution of 1848.

Goodbye to Charlotte and Daniel

When I first began thinking about the CHARLOTTE EDGERTON MYSTERIES series, I decided I would follow in Margaret Fuller's footsteps and try to discover what life was like for Americans living through the 1840s. The journey has been fascinating and Charlotte and Daniel proved to be excellent companions along the way. After ten years of growing and exploring the world, they are ready to return to America and continue their lives, raise their family, and pursue their dreams.

Earlier Books in the Charlotte Edgerton Mystery Series

A Death in Utopia: A Charlotte Edgerton Mystery

Charlotte Edgerton, a young teacher, and her friend Daniel Gallagher, an ambitious Irish immigrant, work together to solve the mysterious death of a handsome young minister at the Utopian community of Brook Farm. The year is 1842, a time of radical social experimentation. Brook Farm was planned as a community where farmers and fiddlers could live together in harmony, sharing labor, art, and ideas. This beautiful dream almost worked, but Utopia is hard to build as these idealists discovered when the swirling passions of jealousy, resentment, and clashing ideas destroyed the peace of the New England countryside. Local farmers were suspicious, slave catchers came through searching for abolitionists and radicals, and immigrants threatened to replace American laborers. What was the explosive force that shattered this bold experiment? Can harmony be restored? This perceptive mystery story mingles history with conjecture.

Death Visits a Bawdy House: A Charlotte Edgerton Mystery

When Charlotte Edgerton, moves from staid Boston to bustling New York City in 1843, she finds the crowds on Broadway thrilling. She is young, idealistic, and in love with crusading newspaperman, Daniel Gallagher. But when first one and then another of the glamorous "sporting girls" who work in the city's famous brothels are murdered, Charlotte becomes aware of the darkness that lurks behind the bright glow of Manhattan. In a city where abolitionists are not popular and suspicion of free blacks runs high, the arrest of a black man for these crimes inflames much of the city. Charlotte discovers that police can be prejudiced, politicians are not always honest, and kindness can lead to danger. Will she be able to find safety for herself and end the terror gripping women throughout the city?

Death Calls at the Palace: A Charlotte Edgerton Mystery

When Charlotte and Daniel move to London in 1846, they see poverty everywhere. Barefoot children sell flowers in the street for a few pennies. Revolutionaries demand a more equal society and threaten to kill their young Queen. This is far from the gracious society Charlotte had imagined. Worst of all, her younger brother Tom is being drawn into political agitation that leads to violence and perhaps death.

London is crowded with impoverished immigrants from famine-stricken Ireland and when one of them—a young kitchen maid—dies in a tragic fire, Charlotte believes it was no accident, although the police scoff at her suspicions. Then the young wife of a friend is kidnapped and Charlotte finds herself in danger as she struggles to discover who is responsible. Society seems determined to protect the rich and powerful and to punish those who rebel against England's rigid class system. It is only when Queen Victoria herself is confronted by a dangerous mob that questions are asked. Will justice ever be found?

www.ingramcontent.com/pod-product-compliance
Lightning Source LLC
Chambersburg PA
CBHW071142170626
46809CB00002B/733